GHOST BOYS

SHENAAZ NANJI

MAWENZI
HOUSE

We acknowledge the support of the Canada Council for the Arts for our publishing program. We also acknowledge support from the Government of Ontario through the Ontario Arts Council.

Cover design by Susan Chafe
Cover photo courtesy of Mikal Hockley
Author photo: D'Angelo Photography

Library and Archives Canada Cataloguing in Publication

Nanji, Shenaaz, author

Ghost boys / Shenaaz Nanji.

Issued in print and electronic formats.

ISBN 978-1-988449-13-5 (softcover).—ISBN 978-1-988449-23-4 (HTML)

I. Title.

PS8577.A573G46 2017   jC813'.54   C2017-904411-7

C2017-904412-5

Printed and bound in Canada by Coach House Printing

Mawenzi House Publishers Ltd.
39 Woburn Avenue (B)
Toronto, Ontario M5M 1K5
Canada

www.mawenzihouse.com

With love to my son Astrum and daughter Shaira

Contents

The Arabian Sea Area

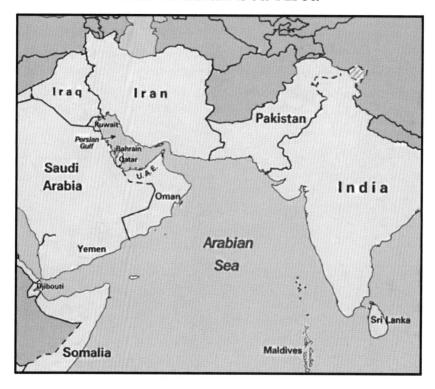

Didi's Homecoming

Guj, India (2004)

Munna was on the last set of his hundred push-ups when a screeching bird crashed into the rusty window grill outside. Crows were the harbingers of doom, but to Munna's relief this bird was not a crow—unless white crows existed.

With every rise of a push-up, he glimpsed on the wall before him the dappled dancing patterns of the shadows cast by the branches of the Neem tree outside. All the walls were stained with soot and grime—he made a mental note to clean them. Nothing would escape his elder sister's sharp eyes.

The bird flew across to the Neem tree and came crashing at the window again, and then back and forth it went, repeating its madness. *Bonk-bonk-bonk.* Silly bird, he thought. No way could it peck holes into his joy. Lost in his dreamworld, Munna imagined himself as Salman Khan, the actor, always risking his life to save others; he did have Salu's smile, but when would he get those amazing six-pack abs?

"Bhaiya," his sister, Meena, said, holding up against her slender neck a paper necklace she had cut from an old *Femina* magazine. "Nice, no?"

Munna sat up, sweat streaming down his face. "I'll get a solid gold one for you on your Big Day," he said, though not sure how he would manage to do it. Meena, however, stretched her list of desirables: "And matching earrings and bangles and a nice purse . . ."

Their one-room flat in the *chawl* or tenement-house was steaming hot. Ma, who catered meals for a living, was cooking a special meal for Didi's homecoming, following her wedding last night. Over the charcoal stove was a big black pan of sizzling curry, on the floor were plates of *aloo gobi*, *bhindi*, *parathas*, and mango pudding, Didi's favorite.

Didi's actual name was Asha, Hope, but to him she was Didi, elder sister. As the brother of the bride, Munna would welcome the newly-wed couple home. And as they stepped inside, his other sisters, Reshma and Meena would throw rose petals to welcome them. Ma would bless them and they'd eat the special meal.

The angry bird crashed once more against the window again, this time with more force, thrashing its white wings and screeching like a banshee. The bowl in Reshma's hands fell, scattering the rose petals on the cement floor.

"Oh God!" Ma cried out, pressing her hands over her mouth. This could mean bad luck.

"It's fine, Ma." Munna went and sat down beside his nervous mother, pressing his cheek against hers. "The silly bird's blind as a bat."

"Ha, its pecking at its reflection," observed Meena with a chuckle.

Reshma began to sweep the floor. Munna ducked his head out the window to wave the bird away. A wetness plopped on his arm. He wiped the insult with the rag, when there came a knock on the door.

Meena opened the door and to Munna's immense

2

surprise, Uncle Suraj waddled in, his large flat feet crammed inside a dainty pair of gold-embroidered *mojri*, swaying from side to side, one hand on the umbrella, the other holding Didi's arm.

Munna gaped. Why had their meddling uncle brought Didi? And, why was she still in her red bridal sari? And . . . and where was the groom, his brother-in-law, Raju? Didi's gaze was downcast, the red powder streak of *sindoor* in her hair-parting, denoting her married status, was missing.

Ma came forward. "Bhai-Jaan, what is the meaning of this?"

"Sister-ji," said Uncle, with a sorry look, "Didi has been returned."

"I'm sorry." Didi put her head on Ma's chest and sobbed.

"My dear girl," said Ma, putting her hand over Didi's head.

Munna's hands balled into angry fists. "I'll kill that stupid Raju."

"Shhh," said Ma. "It's our kismet. What is, will be."

Uncle said that Didi's father-in-law had called him to take Didi back because he felt insulted at the measly wedding gifts received, especially as his son was an engineer. Uncle mimicked the father-in-law. "*Where is the big-screen TV?*" "*Where is the gold jewellery? No gold, no bride.*"

Munna gripped at his marble collection in his pocket. A rejected bride was a disgrace to the family regardless of the circumstances. He knew that dowry was illegal in India. The law stated: *Dowry is a two-way street: unless there is a giver there can be no taker, so both could be persecuted.* Still, to give Didi a good start, Ma had borrowed money from Uncle and given her in-laws a refrigerator, a sewing machine, a set of stainless-steel utensils, and a pressure cooker.

They were all filled with a deep sense of shame and grief.

On top of that, Munna felt an intense anger. Was this one more outcome of the curse he had been born with?

They sat down on the bedsheet on the floor to eat. Didi excused herself and left with a bundle of clothes to wash. Uncle was the only one who ate.

The meal over, Munna went to look for Didi. Past the hallway—their flat was on the topmost floor of the six-storey *chawl*—down sixty-six fat stone steps into the dark bowels of the building to the communal bathrooms on the ground floor shared by all the tenants. Didi's beaded slippers lay outside the plumbing room that led to the wash area outside. He smiled: he would surprise her. Creeping into the dark, dank room, past a hot-water tank, he almost tripped over a fallen stool—oops—and bumped into a pair of legs dangling in the air.

He looked up at the network of water pipes in the ceiling. Suspended from one of them, Didi swung pendulum-like, head fallen on one side, neck coiled in the red bridal sari, two limp eyes staring down at him pitifully.

He screamed, but no sound came, except for a bird caw-cawing lustily outside.

The Cremation

As always it was the darkest just before dawn. Munna saw flecks of electric-blue fireflies twinkling in the darkness and heard the crickets chirping as he stood barefoot and bare-chested on the river bank, where the townsfolk of Guj held cremations. He wore a white loincloth, a pot of holy water cradled in the crook of his arm for the rite. Was Didi really gone? He dared not look down at the pyre on which her body lay.

The breeze prickled his chest, limbs, and scalp, which was shaved clean for the ritual. He was glad the dark hid him. He could make out the silhouettes of the few mourners huddled around him. Ma and his sisters were home since women did not attend cremations. If only he had his marbles; they were his prayer beads, but the loincloth he wore had no pockets.

The mourners chanted prayers in low, sorrowful tones.

Still, Munna did not dare look down. His toes curled tight as a baby's fist. No god would damn a day-old bride. Unless . . . unless the curse that was on him was more powerful than the wishes of a god. His chest heaved. *He was bad, bad, bad.* If only he could run away from the bad inside him.

Duty first. His duty was to set alight the pyre when the sun rose. A male close relation had to carry out this rite. His father had run away long ago, leaving him as the only male member in his family. He gazed at the sky, intrigued as to why some things in life were sure and predictable: the sun would rise, no matter what. Sure enough, a weak lemony sun rose above the clay-tiled roofs of the distant buildings as the sky unfolded her silk-sari pleats of saffron and sherbet, the color of new beginnings. Any moment, the roosters would announce the new day.

Instead, red-breasted bulbuls, perched on the branch of the enormous mango tree nearby, sang, *chic-chok chic-chok*, giving him the courage to lower his gaze.

The pyre was veiled by sandalwood smoke. Peeking through the smoke, a pile of twigs draped with marigold petals and . . . and a pair of dainty feet stuck out, soles stained with henna, the sensual wedding decoration said to please the groom and guarantee marital bliss.

Baba-ji, the old priest who had tried to remove his curse long ago, poured molten golden ghee on the pyre, lit the holy *kusha* twig, and gave it to Munna.

"Go round three times," he instructed with a counter-clockwise gesture.

Munna nodded. Everything was backwards in death. He firmed up his grip on the pot and dragged his leaden legs onward in the first circle round the pyre. Didi was barely five feet tall, but she had been big in his life. Long ago, she once caught sight of a few boys making fun of the steel hoop in his ear. She took out a bottle of red chilies from her shopping basket and made to throw it at them and they scuttled away. Now she was gone.

In his second time round the pyre, Didi's wedding ceremony rewound in his mind. She looked dazzling in her red sari, which was embroidered with silver *zari*, her face adorned with strings of jasmines, behind which peeked out her large kohl-rimmed eyes. He had offered a branch of mango leaves to Didi as a symbol of fertility, whispering, *I hope to be a proud uncle of eleven nephews, enough for a cricket team.* He was one of the best batsmen in the cricket team at school. She had smiled coyly. Then the bridal couple rose. Didi's sari was tied to the groom's *kurta* and the couple circled the fire clockwise, pledging vows of commitment to each other . . .

Someone waved a knife at him.

"Beta, the rounds are over," Uncle Suraj said with a smile, his false teeth flashing. His sequined cap hid his baldness, but not the hair in his ears that had to be the longest in town; the faux gold buttons on his *sherwani*, as big as goose eggs, twinkled.

Munna held out the pot for Uncle, who stabbed it with his knife.

The holy water spilled out. Munna dropped the pot to symbolize the release of Didi's soul, the crash echoing eerily in his ears, recalling to his mind the spooky monsoon night long ago when his father had flung his beer bottle against the wall and run away, never to return. He tried to push the bad memory back. If only he had a pocket to hide his pain. Pockets were neat. Pockets kept things clean. If he was the Creator, he would ensure everyone had deep pockets—a grief pocket, a shame pocket, a fear pocket, a dream pocket . . . then their feelings would stay put. Not run into each other. Life would be clutter-free.

He lifted his gaze a little. Hai, the mourners were waiting for him to light the pyre. He raised the flare, his red *rakhi* dangling on his wrist. Didi had tied it during the festival when brothers and sisters express their love and duty to each other.

He had failed to protect Didi. *Failed-failed.* The word tolled like temple bells in his ears. Chilled to the marrow, he began to shake like a leaf.

"Give me the flare," said Uncle.

7

"I'll do it," said Munna.

He lowered the flare and lit the pyre. The twigs flared and snapped, red tongues of flames dancing. Baba-ji stoked the fire with a long pole to keep it burning. The fire would burn for a few hours, after which Uncle had arranged for the ashes to be picked up and dispersed in the River Ganges. Munna wrenched himself away from the flaming pyre and headed home, carrying along with him the echo of the popping and crackling of bones and the odor of burning flesh, his curse taunting him: *You can't beat me.*

He ran down the alley, the rocky ground jabbing his bare feet, past a cow resting by the side of the road, then cut across the cricket field until he reached home. Reaching the stairs, he sank into his hidey-hole, where he had played Barrier in his dark moments since he was six.

Born after three girls, he was said to be cursed. When he was just over three, his drunken father ran away, and Munna fell seriously sick. Doctors failed to treat him, so Ma had taken him to the priest to remove the curse.

Old Baba-ji had shaken his head and said, *Daughter, you can't escape the law. God gave you a son after three daughters and that curse will remain with you forever. The curse is like the car rolling down the hill. You can't stop it. But I will try to alleviate his suffering.*

Munna remembered feeling queasy as he put his head on Ma's lap and she pulled up his t-shirt. Chanting mantras, Baba-ji took a needle and made a tick mark on his forehead, stomach, and big toe; he made a cross on a *paan*-leaf and told Ma to place it at a busy crossroad. He pierced Munna's ear and changed his name from Anand to Munna, telling Ma that this way the curse would be led astray.

Now Didi was dead. It must be his fault. The curse was back.

Barrier

In the days following Didi's cremation, a fog of shame and scandal hung over the family. Ma received fewer orders to cater for, as if the food she cooked now was tainted. Gossip buzzed like hungry flies gorging on a ripe-rotten guava in their back alley. People's looks said: *So sorry.* They knew about Munna's curse and their runaway father, and Didi's death had further eroded their *aabroo*, honor.

On Sunday morning Munna awoke with a groggy head. He struggled in the darkness of his mind, groping for something to hold on to, anything to return him to the world as it had been when Didi was alive. He picked up his marbles and inspected them: crystals, devil's eye, galaxies, swirlies, oilies. What a collection, they could be the world's rarest. Glass globes rounded to perfection. If only he could crawl inside one of them and touch the rainbow swirls floating like clouds in heaven. He flung an old marble against the wall to crack it.

"Prince, breakfast's ready," Meena said and sprinkled cold water on his face.

He went to sit beside Ma on the floor, and began nibbling warm *poori*. Ma was frying onions on the big black pan over the charcoal stove, her face gleaming with sweat and soot. The red *bindi* on her forehead signified that she was still married. *A lie.* Her husband, his father, was likely dead. They had never heard from him. But Ma held on to her fantasy that her knight in *kurta* would return. Of late, she had begun to observe a ritual of fasting for a whole day, as a sacrifice to the gods for ensuring her husband's long life.

His gaze shifted to his sisters. Soon they too would marry. Reshma, soft and self-effacing, might be bullied by her in-laws, but Meena with her sharp tongue would be fine.

"Nice?" asked Reshma.

Before he could reply, they had a visitor. Lalita, the fashionable wife of a rich businessman, hurriedly spoke with Ma at the door, and left.

Ma shut the door and turned around. "The big order is cancelled," she said in a teary voice.

Lalita was their prized customer. Already, they were knee-deep in debt to Uncle for Didi's wedding expense. Munna did odd jobs after school, serving tea at Viram Bhai's roadside stall and cleaning Kanji Bhai's restaurant, but that barely paid his school fees. He worried. How would they pay Reshma's and Meena's dowries when they married? If his sisters grew too old to get grooms, they would grow old without families . . . or follow Didi's fate? A noose hung around their necks.

He walked over to the window and gazed into the back alley, where boys from the neighborhood were playing marbles. One of them, Raja, held up his fingers to show the devil's horn, teasing Munna about his curse; the others laughed.

Munna gritted his teeth. Did Raja think he ruled the world just because his father, who worked in the Middle East, brought home electronic gifts? Once Raja had let him play his new video game. But when Munna advanced to a higher level, Raja had stopped the game and wouldn't play with him.

Munna fingered the marbles in his pocket, and the discarded cigarette lighter he had picked up on the street last week. He smiled grimly. It didn't work, but he'd make good use of it.

Down the stairs he ran, the marbles clinking in his pocket. When he was young, he was the best marble shooter in Guj. All the players would crowd around him, shouting, "Look, he's double-jointed!" Indeed, he could freakishly bend his fingers far back.

Now, nudging fifteen, he no longer played marbles but collected them by playing Barrier. Of course, no one in his family knew about this. Barrier felt wrong, but it energized him. It was the only thing he could do to be in control.

He paused on the bottom floor to practice his skill. Pitching his marbles one by one into the air, he caught them with his other hand, then raised a leg, threw them under and caught them as they arched over his head. He grinned at himself.

A shuffling. He pocketed his marbles and wedged into his hidey-hole, the dark space under the stairs. Little Bilu was coming up the steps, his eyes big and bright, like a frightened cat at night.

"Hey, Bilu, who's your favorite actor?"

Bilu pointed a crooked finger at him. Munna laughed and pressed a marble into the tiny hand. Bilu toddled up the steps as fast as he could.

More footsteps. Munna's eyes, accustomed to the dark, spotted Raja, and he stretched out his long legs across the stair. Nobody dared cross his barrier without paying toll. Often, the boys gave up whatever their pockets held—marbles, sweets, chewing gum. The smart ones paid at once; the stupids got elbow pokes in their rib cages, and the rare brave one got the Chinese burn—Munna would grab the kid's forearm with both his hands and twist them in the opposite direction to give his victims a ripping-burning sensation.

Munna stretched out an open palm. "Pay up for safe passage."

Raja sneered in return. "Hey, Cursed One, these are not your stairs."

Munna took out the cigarette lighter from his pocket and thrust it near the boy's crotch. "Say that once more and I'll . . ."

Raja dropped a marble into Munna's palm and quickly fled up the stairs, as did the others who had followed. A feeling of power surged through Munna. He was a force to reckon with. Soon he would be strong enough to fight his curse. He pumped his arms to demonstrate.

Searching for a Job

M unna finished his morning *puja* at their home shrine, reluctantly bowing to the image of Durga Ma, the Mother of Creation. He knew every weapon in her ten arms. She had killed demons that no man could, but had done nothing to save Didi. He slung his knapsack upon his shoulder, bade farewell to his family, and left for school. At every step, his shoes pinched his toes. His feet seemed to grow by the day. Didi came floating alongside, her long braids flicking at the waist: *Elephant Feet*, said the disembodied voice. They always teased each other, and then they knocked foreheads and she'd say: *Bhoot ya buddhi?* Foolish or wise?

An image of a rope around the necks of his sisters Reshma and Meena flashed into his mind. His chest tightened, he could barely breathe. Kicking clods of dirt on his way he detoured, trudged across the field toward the river bank to the site of Didi's cremation. There he sat down under the mango tree to contemplate on his family's future. He heard Didi's chuckle: *Need an awakening, little Buddha?*

He leaned his back against the trunk and rolled his marbles in his palm. Ma would be upset that he had missed school. She bragged about him to everyone: *My son is number one in class. He will be a big doctor like Dr Mehta.* But deep in a secret chamber of his heart he yearned to be a famous actor, a hero.

He imagined himself as Salman Khan in a red collarless jacket, standing atop a moving bus, shaking his hips, the crowd going wild. Not only would he earn tons of money, he'd be a *bada aadmi*, a man respected and idolized. Fame would erase shame, bring honor to his family. There were stories of ordinary men who became famous stars. Like Akshay Kumar and SRK. Almost every chawl had a story of a survivor who became a thriver.

He pocketed his marbles, staring vacantly at an overhanging branch on which a yellow mango shone like the moon. Mango was Didi's favorite fruit. When he was little he'd throw stones to down the mangoes, then tuck them under his t-shirt, and run to Didi.

He rose and, grabbing a low tree branch, climbed up the tree. When he was close to the shiny mango, he lowered its branch towards him and plucked it. Firm and plump. He sat on a fork in the branches, his feet swinging beneath him, and bit into the mango. Sticky juice dribbled down his chin as he recalled a story that Didi had told him once.

One day a mischievous saint offered a mango to a couple, saying whoever ate the fruit would be blessed with eternal wisdom. The couple had two sons, and they both desired the mango. At a loss, they asked the saint whom they should give the mango to. He said: The first one to go around the universe three times should get the fruit. The first son mounted a peacock and flew around the universe. The second son circled around his parents three times and won the mango.

He looked at the sticky stone of the fruit in his hand. His universe was his family. He'd win the mango for them. Reshma and Meena would *not* follow the way of Didi. He made a plan. Placing his right hand on his chest, he swore to choose death before dishonor. *In the name of the gods, I will restore my family's honor, and secure their future, no matter what.*

He jumped off the tree and ran home to tell his family.

It was quiet at home. Reshma and Meena had left for the market. Ma was sweeping the floor.

"Ma," Munna said breathlessly. "I'm going to look for a full-time job."

Ma's face hardened. She stared at the broom in her hand as if there were something special about it, then set it against the wall and turned to him.

"Beta," she said in an anxious voice. "Son, there's no future without education, unless you want to wash clothes or run errands."

"I'm a boy, Ma. I'll rough it out." he said. "What about Reshma and Meena? They are of marriageable age, but we don't have enough for their dowries. And how will we pay Uncle's loan? What if your business slips further?"

"I'll fast all week," she said. "God is sure to bless us."

Munna recoiled. Poor Ma always bribed the gods, yet they did not help her. He would not relinquish his family's honor to the play of the gods. He would make his own fate. He took hold of her arm. "Ma, we must make an effort to save ourselves, or we'll be on the streets." Ma shut her eyes in horror at the thought. "Do you want that? Do you want Reshma and Meena to suffer Didi's fate?"

Ma opened her eyes and shook her head, and he gave her a hug.

Munna scoured the noisy streets of Guj from morning till dusk begging for employment. Motilal, the cobbler, offered him to set up a shoe-shine stand as long as he paid half his earnings as rent. Kanji Bhai the restaurant owner, and Viram

Bhai the tea-kiosk owner, offered him full-time jobs, but the income would barely pay for their ration at home, and Munna turned them down.

One afternoon he sank in frustration on the curb, which was packed with vendors selling everything under the sun, when he spotted a familiar dome-bellied man galumphing across the street with the help of his umbrella. Uncle Suraj. Munna always thought that Uncle was a braggart; his stories—ninety parts fairy tale, ten parts truth—could turn a donkey feverish. But now as he waited for Uncle to pass, an idea flashed into his brain. He stood up and ran to greet the man. Folding his hands respectfully, he greeted, "*Namaste Kaka-ji.*"

Uncle's henna-dyed brows shot up like question marks. "What are you doing here, beta?"

"I quit school," Munna said.

"Quit?" said Uncle, looking horrified, as though Munna had committed a robbery. "Quit?" Uncle repeated. He clutched Munna's arm to steady himself. "Does your Ma know?"

Munna nodded. "Kaka-ji, can you find me a nice job?" Uncle's grip on Munna's arm tightened and he felt a burst of energy shooting through the pudgy fingers.

"*Bilkul,* Absolutely. What kind of job you want, beta?"

"Any. I'll work hard, dirty my hands, put in crazy hours, do what it takes, as long as I'm paid well."

Uncle tapped his umbrella tip on the pavement in deep thought, then looked up with a wide smile. "Kaka-ji is blessed with rich friends. I will ask them."

"Thank you, Kaka-ji," said Munna.

"No problem," Uncle said, displaying his gleaming false teeth and finally letting Munna's arm go.

Munna skipped away, singing all the way home. Didi would be amused that of all people he had asked Uncle for help.

Bhoot or Buddhi? He heard her voice.

He laughed. Didi could tease him even from up there.

Sweet News

Munna slunk into his hidey-hole at the bottom of the stairs. Another week had crawled by, still he had not found a good paying job. Should he go to Mumbai, the city of dreams, and try to become a movie star, like Amitabh or Salman?

Tup-tup, tup-tup came a sound up the stairs. Munna peered outside.

Uncle was coming up the fat stone steps tapping his umbrella. He ran into Munna and shrieked: "What you do, beta? Hiding like a rat?" He caught Munna's elbow, leaning his ample weight on him. "How big and strong you have grown, boy," he panted.

Munna puffed up with pride. So Uncle had noticed his biceps bulging from his vest; he had earned them by carrying bags of potatoes, rice, and flour for Ma every week.

"Come, come, Kaka-ji has sweet news for you," Uncle said, still gripping Munna's arm, nearly squashing it as he hauled himself up the steps, breathless. Munna's heart raced in anticipation. When they reached the flat, he held the door open. Uncle hurried inside.

Ma hastened to pull the edge of her *dupatta* over her head. Uncle joined his hands in a pranam. "*Wa-wa* Sister-ji. Like Saira Banu." Ma frowned at the reference to the actress. Her grey hair was tied into a tight bun above the nape of her neck, her face etched with deep lines, her *kameez*, faded and threadbare. Ma's turmeric-stained nails couldn't be more unlike the nails of an actress.

Reshma and Meena greeted Uncle politely and went to sit next to Munna on the floor, one on each side. Uncle plopped into the only chair, which gave a squeak, and naughty Meena nudged Munna and giggled. Uncle saw them and shifted again, making the chair squeak more loudly, as if to clarify that it was the chair, not him.

Uncle leaned towards Ma on the floor, secretively, but his voice was loud enough for all to hear. "Sister-ji, I worry about your girls. What will happen when they marry?" He shook his head to commiserate.

Reshma and Meena lowered their heads in embarrassment. A hush fell over the room. *If only Ma didn't breathe so loud*, thought Munna, as she twisted the two ends of her *dupatta* together.

"Don't worry, Sister," said Uncle. "I'm here for you."

Munna wished Uncle would hurry up and spill his sweet news. But Ma got up and brought chai, so the tea took precedence. Uncle blew across the surface of the tea, savoring every sip. Finally, he tipped the cup to down the last dreg, and said with a smile, "Sister, I have found a nice job for Munna."

Munna rose on his knees. "Where Kaka-ji? What job? What salary?"

Uncle beamed, flashing his false teeth. "Patience, beta. Patience bears sweet flowers." His gaze flipped back and forth from Ma to Munna. "Each month you will earn . . ." he paused for dramatic effect, then threw the bomber. "Three thousand rupees!" He slapped his thighs gleefully.

Munna's heart leaped. To earn all that money! It was a

dream come true. Reshma and Meena could get happily married. He exchanged incredulous glances with them. Just two years of work would suffice to pay for their dowries, after which he would finish his schooling . . . He had been wrong about Uncle; the man had really come through. "Thank you Kaka-ji!" he said, as did Reshma and Meena, but Ma said nothing.

"Time to celebrate," said Uncle, eyeing the bright saffron coils of *jalebi* on the counter with interest. Ma offered the plate to everyone. Uncle grabbed a piece. It was Munna's favorite sweet, but full of excitement, he politely declined.

Ma cleared her throat. "Go on, Bhai-jaan, tell us more about Munna's job."

Uncle licked his sticky fingers. "He will work for my rich friend, the Sheikh of Deeba."

Munna was dumbstruck. Deeba was in the Middle East! Before he could respond, Ma rose angrily to her feet, like Goddess Kali facing a demon. "No, Bhai-jaan, no!" she said. Her *dupatta* slipped off her head, but she made no effort to pull it up. "Munna will not leave home. *Kabhi nahi*, never ever!"

"Sorry, Sister," Uncle said in a wounded tone. "I came here first because one shares sweets with dear ones, no?"

Of course, Munna didn't want to leave home. His fingers rubbed against the marbles in his pocket, feeling their warmth for comfort. But he thought, Middle East was close to India. Didn't Raja's father work there? He came home every six months. The plan seemed feasible. "Go on, Kaka-ji," he said, despite Ma's glare.

Uncle's gaze unlocked from Ma and settled on Munna. "Beta, the oil boom's transformed the desert into nirvana. They call Deeba *Sonapuri*, city of gold."

"Kaka-ji, what do I need to do?" asked Munna.

Uncle smiled. "*Bilkul* nothing. Absolutely nothing. The Sheikh's men will train you prim and proper. They hire hundreds of workers from all over the world—cleaners to clean the hundred-room palace, cooks, drivers, tutors to teach their children. The Sheikh has money spilling out of his ears. He'll pay your fare, boarding, lodging, training, everything."

Oh, to work in a palace! Munna's mind dwelled on the throne rooms of the palaces in *Arabian Nights*, where Persian rugs hung on every wall and beautiful girls fanned the king with peacock feathers . . . He didn't mind even if he had to work as a lowly servant. He looked up expectantly at Ma, but she looked upset, her hands joined together in front of her, the worry lines deep on her face.

"Opportunity doesn't knock twice," said Uncle. "The monkey who misses the branch falls."

Munna was sure Uncle was right. The gods had heard him at last. He felt a sudden strength surge inside him. He turned to Ma. "Kaka-ji is right. I will earn good money. Reshma and Meena will get nice grooms . . ." he stopped, for Ma was trembling.

"Bapu left." Her voice quavered. "Then Didi." She choked. "Now *you*?"

"Ma, I'll be back! I'm not like that loser."

"Don't call your Bapu that. You were his sweet little boy."

Munna scowled. He had nothing but anger for his runaway father. Where was he when Munna fell sick and was close to dying? When Didi got married? When they needed a shoulder to cry on?

"Ma, he's as good as dead. If not, I'll bust every bone in his body . . ."

He stopped as Ma's hands flew to her face and she began to cry.

Munna felt awful. He ought to keep his big mouth shut. Didi was right when she teased him about his tongue that flew out faster than a chameleon's. He hadn't meant to hurt Ma.

Predictably, his uncle butted in at this moment, pointing his umbrella-tip at him like a gun. "Your Ma's right, absolutely," he said. "Your Bapu may have one or two bad habits, but his heart must be good for your Ma to care for him still." He gave a concerned look at Ma. "Sorry, Sister, I came to help only. After all, your family's my family, *na*? Don't worry, I will take Munna with me."

Ma's lips puckered. Munna was afraid she would cry again. He picked Uncle's umbrella from the floor and handed it to him. "Kaka-ji, we'll let you know. Thank you for your kind offer."

"Oh, it's nothing," said Uncle. He rose heavily to his feet and waddled out the door with the aid of his umbrella.

Over the next few days, the more Munna thought about his job, the more he desired it. He could save his family's future and honor, become the good son and brother his family could be proud of. Besides, he might even rid himself of his curse.

Every day he would talk to Ma about the job, try to convince her, but she simply pursed her lips, refusing to be drawn into the subject. One day he had a bright idea. He asked: "Ma, if you win a lottery will you claim the prize?"

"Hmmm," responded Ma thoughtfully. "Not if I'm going to lose the bigger prize."

"Ma, Reshma and Meena will marry with *dham-dhoom*, in high style! I'll buy you a new gas stove!"

Ma shook her head, clasping her palms together as though squeezing a dry lemon.

A few days later he tried the desperation tactic. "Ma, if we're caught in a raging current in the midst of a deep river, will you let your children drown or push them aboard a lifeboat?"

Ma frowned. "Since when did you learn to talk in such a colorful language, like Bapu?"

Munna exchanged a smile with Reshma and Meena. He was winning.

Later, as Ma came out of the kitchen, he said, "Ma, I will mail you my paycheck each month."

Ma smiled weakly then gave a soft sigh, which sounded like air slowly leaking out of a bicycle tire. "Beta, the truth is I don't want to lose you."

"Ma. I promise you I'll be back. I want to finish school, and go to college. I have big dreams."

Reshma held Ma's hand, and Meena urged, "Let Bhaiya go, mother. We're here with you."

"Come near, beta," said Ma. Her yellow fingertips brushed his face from his forehead, down to his cheeks, to his dimpled chin, as though she were memorizing his features. "Go if you must. We will wait for you."

Munna gave his mother a tight hug.

The next day, when Uncle came home for "chai and chat," Munna gave him the news.

Uncle raised his umbrella in a sign of victory. "We better leave before the job offer expires. I will help you apply for your passport." He gave Munna a thump on his back. "You are brave. Your Bapu would be proud of you."

Munna beamed, but felt nervous inside. He had never gone away before.

Never left home.

Never left his family.

Never left Guj.

Never left Mother India.

He dug his hands into his pockets, seeking comfort in the feel of his marbles.

Farewell

Soon everyone and their cow seemed to know of Munna's job in the city of gold. When he passed by Raja and his friends, they gave him envious looks. Uncle told Munna that he must look tip-top when they met the Sheikh, so he took Munna to Royal Emporium and bought him wrinkle-free polyester pants and a blue button-down checked shirt.

"Thank you, Kaka-ji," said Munna in a quavering voice, moved at receiving these expensive gifts.

"It's nothing," said Uncle.

All week long, Munna sang praises of his Uncle.

Munna woke up before sun-up, excited about his Big Journey. It was an occasion of firsts—first time leaving his home and family, first time sailing in a ship. From his knapsack he removed his thick, dog-eared textbooks of math, science, and English, and stuffed it with his personal effects. He put on his new clothes and shoes. The stiff collar of his shirt chafed his long neck, leaving a red rash. Small beans.

He checked out himself in the mirror, stared incredulously at his reflection. If only Didi could see him.

At breakfast, nobody talked or ate much. Despite his excitement, he had a heavy feeling in his heart. When it was time to say goodbye, he was afraid Ma would make a scene, but to his surprise, she kissed his forehead calmly and gave him a neatly folded shawl.

"Stay warm," she said. "Come back quickly and tell us all about the city of gold."

The shawl was bright with many colors. Munna had watched it grow every night in Ma's hands as she knitted it. It had a lotus design in one corner. Ma put a lotus into everything she knitted, for good luck. He took the shawl, relishing its softness and tucked it carefully into his knapsack. Then he bent down to touch Ma's feet for her blessings. Ma pulled him up by his arms and held him close.

When his sisters embraced him, he could hardly look into their faces. "We'll miss you," Reshma said in a heart-broken voice, and Meena tweaked his nose playfully. "Don't turn big-headed and forget us." Once more, she went through the long list of things she wanted: saris, slippers, purses, jewelry. He wanted to tease her, but his heart was full with so many feelings squeezing his chest that he could only nod and give a weak smile. A strong voice admonished him: *Be strong. Duty before passion.*

Slinging his knapsack onto his shoulder, he left for the bus stop, where Uncle was waiting. He waved his umbrella, the wizard's wand. He had spun magic out of thin air. "You look first class, beta. First class."

Munna carried Uncle's steel trunk into the waiting bus destined for the seaport, which was sixty kilometres away. The bus was crowded, and Uncle squeezed himself into a seat already packed with people. Munna stood in the aisle, holding on to the overhead handrail for support, careful not to rub his new clothes against anything that would stain them. On their way they passed paddy and bright marigold fields where the cows roamed freely, and little villages where boys played cricket and men sat around idly under a tree.

It took about an hour and half to reach the seaport. They alighted at the bus stop and made their way to the shore.

"Our ship," Uncle cried, pointing to the *Star of India* anchored in the harbor, the name painted upon its side in white. Its black hull was peppered with rust spots and a flag on its stern flapped with pride. A mix of excitement and nervousness fizzed inside Munna. He was going to sail in a ship. A real ship, on this vast blue ocean that stretched mysteriously before him, beyond which lay all the other countries of the world. There were a few fishing boats scattered close by in the water. A vision of his past suddenly flashed into his brain. He was sitting on his father's lap, a toddler with star-struck eyes, gazing at a chocolate lake—a muddy ditch in their back alley. His father was cutting up old newspapers and folding the pieces into small paper boats. One by one, he handed the boats to Munna, who pushed them into the lake, blowing hard at them. The boats sailed like a brood of baby ducklings. It was magical, until it began to rain and the boats sank.

A loud horn jerked Munna to the present. Uncle caught his arm. "Time to board." They went down the gangway into the ship, threading their way on to the main deck jammed with crates stacked up high and covered in orange tarpaulin. Uncle said they contained rice, flour, and potatoes. Of course, nothing grew in the desert, so most of the food was imported from India.

The ship sailed slowly out of the quay. It was a clear day, and soon all Munna could see was the blue of the sea and the blue of the sky. His world disappeared, as if nothing he knew existed any more. The only proof of his home were the images in his mind. Ma and his sisters cooking, he playing cricket at school. He pulled out the shawl Ma had given him from his knapsack and put it around his shoulders, inhaling its sandalwood scent.

"Nice," said Uncle, admiring the shawl.

Munna sniffled, his heart as heavy as the ship's anchor, and Uncle wrapped an arm around him. "Don't cry, Beta. They'll be safe and waiting when you return."

"I'm not crying," said Munna, dabbing the drip at the tip of his nose with his hand.

"Come," said Uncle. "Let's check our room."

They went down the steps to the lower deck into the cabin they shared.

The City of God & Gold

Munna stared at the skyline across the water, awed by the glowing lights of tall glass skyscrapers that rose up into the dark night. Below, in the dark water, the reflections twinkled like the decorations at Diwali. Never had he seen such a sight. This was Sonapuri, his destination. Back home most buildings at dawn were dark and squat.

"New Deeba," said Uncle.

The ship suddenly entered a creek crowded with wooden ships with curved sterns and triangular sails. "Old Deeba," said Uncle. "These boats are dhows, they carry cargo to Africa, Far East, China."

There was a sudden quiet and the ship seemed to have stopped moving. Then a whistle screeched to alert the passengers to disembark. Munna slung his knapsack on his shoulder and pulled Uncle's steel trunk out of the gangway. On the shore, they wound around narrow spice-scented alleys, Munna dragging along the trunk. On either side of them were open-air stalls standing jammed next to each other. At the doorways were gunny sacks filled with spices and dried fruit. The stall owners were Indians, and Uncle exchanged jovial greetings with them. Munna smiled in delight. This was just like India!

They left the spice market and entered the Gold Souk.

It was a glittering, shiny place of bright lights. Glass-fronted cabinets displayed the gold jewelry, faceless mannequins looked out at him, wearing thick gold necklaces. Munna's eyes hurt from the glare.

"Kaka-ji, is this real gold?" he asked.

"*Bilkul*, absolutely," Uncle said, shaking his head. "Pure gold. Twenty-four carat gold!"

On Munna's way home, he'd have enough money to buy gifts for his sisters. Reshma would wear a dazzling gold necklace, Meena, dangling gold earrings and a red silk sari with sequins. On the eves of their weddings there would be fireworks and, ah yes! there would be drummers, people dancing on the streets, and the grooms would arrive on horses to claim his sisters. His heart soared to the soulful music of a shehnai.

The lilting call of morning prayers rose from the mosques nearby, breaking his dream. Though he was a Hindu, he closed his eyes momentarily to thank the gods. They kept walking, passing tall office buildings, banks, and stores selling carpets, shoes, and electronics. To his delight, Uncle stopped at a store and bought him a gold wristwatch.

"You are as kind as your good father was. Thank you for looking after me when I was sick on the ship," said Uncle. "The mango never falls far from the tree, no? The watch will help you keep time."

Munna pledged never to show up late for work. "Thank you Kaka-ji," he said solemnly.

"It's nothing," said Uncle.

Arriving at a car-rental agency, Uncle went inside and picked a red van to drive to the Sheikh's palace. Munna sat in the passenger seat, marvelling at the dials on the dashboard. He had never sat in a car before. He felt important. If only Ma and his sisters could see him!

"Time to fuel up our stomachs now," said Uncle. "Hungry?" Munna nodded. They stopped at an Indian restaurant.

Questions plagued Munna's mind like a swarm of bees. He was starting a new life but knew nothing about it.

"Kaka-ji, how far is the Sheikh's palace?"

"An hour or two," said Uncle. "Don't worry. We'll be there before you know it."

"Kaka-ji, is the Sheikh strict?" he asked.

"No, no," said Uncle. "But the Sheikh rewards hard workers with big bonuses."

Munna pledged to work hard, but . . . "Kaka-ji, what if I make mistakes?"

"Save your questions for the ride. Let's eat first."

The waiter brought a tray filled with food. Munna was surprised that it tasted so good. Better than Ma's? No . . . but it tasted good. His uncle filled up his plate again. "Eat, beta, eat," he said. Munna was full, but it was polite to finish everything on his plate. Then Uncle ordered a tall glass of fizzy red soda. "Drink," he said. Munna did so, though the soda tasted funny.

Finally they left for the Sheikh's palace. Munna enjoyed the rush of wind from his half-open car window, as it slapped against his face. Uncle patted his knee, his black stone ring cold and sharp. "Sleep beta, sleep," he said.

Munna nodded. How could he when he had so many questions? He tried to keep his eyes open. But soon his head gently drooped against his car window, and he fell asleep.

Master

Munna awoke with a jolt, causing his knapsack to bounce on his lap. He felt woozy, as if he were on a fast-rotating carousel spinning out of control. Next to him, his uncle steered the car down a lonely road bounded on both sides by a sea of sand. Of course, they were in the desert on their way to see the Sheikh! He glanced at his new watch. Surely, he couldn't have slept the whole way?

"Kaka-ji, are we there?" he asked groggily.

"Rest, beta, rest," said Uncle. "I will wake you up when we reach."

"Yes Kaka-ji," said Munna politely. He leaned his head against his window but his eyes remained open.

Outside, the expanse of land was dotted with scraggly trees, their thorny limbs entwined into tortured, tangled positions. Short spiky plants sprouted here and there. Did fruits and vegetables grow here? He recalled the mango and guava trees back home. Well, he needn't worry. There would be plenty of fruits and vegetables at the Sheikh's palace.

Soon the car slowed, passing a ghostlike settlement consisting of a stall and a gas station. Uncle parked the van. "We have to wait for the Sheikh's man," he said.

Munna nodded, disappointed. Why not the Sheikh himself? Perhaps it was silly to expect such an important man to come to greet them. In a few minutes, a dusty truck approached noisily from the opposite direction and screeched to a stop a short distance away.

"That's him. Stay here, I'll call you," said Uncle. He got out of the car with the support of his umbrella.

Munna watched through the windshield. The truck door flung open and a man stepped out. He was dressed in white Indian *kurta-pyjama*. Oversized dark sunglasses covered much of his face and he carried a stick in one hand. The two men embraced and chatted for a few minutes, then Uncle waved his umbrella at Munna.

Grabbing his knapsack, Munna leaped out of the van. Squinting his eyes against the brilliance of the sun, he walked towards the two men, taking in the scentless dry desert air, his shoes sinking in the soft hot sand that gleamed like gold. Oops, suddenly he was about to fall. His head spun, his legs felt wobbly. Why had he stuffed himself so much?

He stood near Uncle. Shading his eyes with one hand, he looked up at the other man, who also looked Indian. The man pushed his glasses up on his forehead, and seeing his face, Munna stifled an exclamation. He wanted to look away, but couldn't. One side of the face had the mottled look of pink frog skin, the other was normal. It was as if he had two faces.

The man met Munna's frightened stare with a chuckle, exposing a few black teeth. "Don't worry, boy, my burns are not harmful. People do stare at me." His voice was surprisingly soft and melodious.

Munna lowered his gaze, feeling hot with embarrassment. Attached to the man's belt was a coin-purse and next to it a leather sheath with a dagger. Reflexively Munna stepped back, glancing quizzically at his uncle, who nodded, saying, "Beta, Master-ji is your boss."

Munna's gut told him to run away, but he fought the instinct. Where could he run? He joined his palms together in greeting to the man, imagining a fire crackling, burning the poor man's skin and flesh.

The man shook his shepherd's stick furiously at Uncle, his wispy long hair flying like white feathers. "*Moorkh*, you fool, you know I want spring chicks."

Munna caught his breath. The man didn't want him. He'd have to go home empty handed.

Uncle replied softly, "*Yaar*, we're both tired old camels, the gods will soon put us down. This is my last trip, and I've brought you a helper. I swear, he's good."

The man stabbed his stick into the sand, cutting lines upon it, in a jittery nervousness. Everything about him was contradictory. He was tall and strong, yet old and haggard as a grandfather; his expression was defiant, yet tender. He was a mix of god and devil.

Uncle held the man by his scalded arm. "A helper will rest your weary bones. He's smart. Smarter than the crack of your stick, worth your salt and chillies."

The man crossed off each line in the sand, raising a cloud of dust into the air.

"*Yaar*, I was dying in the ship," said Uncle. "This boy saved my life."

"Is that so?" The man looked at Munna with a hint of a smile. and suddenly grabbed Munna's forearm, prodding and pressing as if checking its firmness. The scaly skin scraped Munna's skin, but he didn't squeal.

"Bah!" The man dropped Munna's arm.

Afraid of being rejected, Munna squared up his shoulders and looked up at the man. "Saheb-ji, I'm a hard worker."

"I told you, *yaar*, I told you," Uncle burst out gleefully.

The man's red eyes bore into Munna. "The desert eats the weak. I don't want wimps."

"Saheb-ji, I'm strong," said Munna. He flexed his arm to show his biceps.

"*Acha*, good. Can you live in the desert where the sun can fry you in seconds?"

Munna's breath caught in his throat, but he nodded.

"Can you tame a brood of *junglee*, wild, kids?"

Munna nodded again, and wondered, would he have to babysit the Sheikh's children?

"I told you, I told you," said Uncle, but the man's stare still held Munna's. "Hmm . . ." he said, reassessing Munna's worth. Twirling his stick into the air like an acrobat, he caught it deftly with his other hand. The man was double-jointed like Munna.

"How old are you?" he asked.

"Almost fifteen," said Munna.

"Fifteen," said the man, gazing pensively at the sky for a few seconds, hastening to wipe his blinking eyes with the back of his scarred hand. He pulled out his glasses from his tunic pocket and put them on, but as he did so, his stick fell on the ground.

Munna picked it up and handed it to him. "*Acha*, Good," the man said, clapping Munna on the shoulder. "The gods have willed it. You can be my mule."

Munna cringed. Hello? He did not travel thousands of miles to be the man's mule! But perhaps the man didn't mean that. And he had to be brave for the sake of his family.

"Okay, let's settle it quickly," snapped the man. "I don't have all day."

"*Bilkul yaar*, certainly," said Uncle in his sweet syrupy voice, giving a wide grin.

Munna felt a pang inside him, as the men exchanged

documents that included his passport. Soon Uncle, his last link to his family, would leave. Their journey together had bonded them.

"Wait, Kaka-ji," Munna said, yanking Uncle's sleeve, delaying his departure.

Uncle's eyes fluttered in rapid succession. "I can't, beta. I'll miss the ship back to India. Don't worry. Master-ji will look after you." He gave Munna a quick hug and departed. Reaching the van, he turned around to look one more time at Munna, then he climbed in and drove away, leaving a cloud of dust behind.

"C'mon, little helper." The man slipped on his glasses, his white angelic tunic flapping in the warm wind like a peace flag. He locked his scalded arm into Munna's, and hauled him towards the dusty truck. "Got to hit the road or the noon sun will broil us into kababs."

The Truck Ride

Munna hugged his knapsack against his chest as the truck rattled over the dirt road. Outside his window, the terrain of sparse grass and scattered shrubs changed into a sea of shimmering sand, as though donned in a golden robe. His fingers played with the buckle of his knapsack, snapping, unsnapping.

Master's free hand reached out and smacked Munna's knuckles. "Stop that."

Munna let go the buckle. "Sorry."

"Master-ji," said the man, with both his faces, sternly.

"Master-ji," said Munna obediently, "how far is the Sheikh's palace?"

Master looked queerly at him. "You mean the Sheikh's ousbah?"

Now Munna looked strangely at Master. "Ousbah?"

"Ousbah is a camel farm," said Master. "The Sheikh's camel farm."

Munna knew nothing about camels. He had only seen them passing on country roads back home, pulling loads.

"Don't tell me your uncle didn't tell you?"

Munna shook his head. He felt as if an elephant was sitting on his chest. Uncle had said he'd work at the Sheikh's palace.

"*Kaminey*," Master swore. "*Badmash . . . pukkah badmash.*" Thorough ruffian. Master pressed the accelerator, letting the van bounce wildly over the rutted road.

Outside, nothing but sand, sand, and more sand.

"Don't tell me the *badmash* sold me a bonehead."

Sold? Munna caught his breath. His heart thumped inside him. He pressed down into his seat. *Sold?* It could never be. Uncle would never . . .

Panic assailed him. Run, fool, run, urged a voice inside him. He was always a fast runner, he could easily catch up with Uncle. He couldn't have gone too far. Munna clutched at his knapsack. But then he had a second thought. Perhaps he should find out this man's intentions.

"Saheb . . ." He tried to speak, but choked.

The truck slowed down. Master glanced at him. "You okay?"

Munna nodded, surprised at the man's concern.

"Dry throat, *na*? The desert's quick to choke strangers." Master's free hand reached under his seat, fumbled inside his goat-skin bag, and brought out a water bottle which he tossed on to Munna's lap. "Here."

Munna tried to thank Master, but choked and coughed again.

"Drink," said Master sternly.

Munna unscrewed the bottle and took a few sips. The cool water eased his burning throat. He turned to meet Master's gaze.

"Ah! Do I smell fear?" he said.

Munna was drenched in sweat. He tried to say yes, he was afraid. He struggled to keep his lip from quivering.

Master snorted. "Easy, boy, I'm like your father. Feel free to tell me your fears."

"I was wondering like . . . like . . . like when will you pay me?"

Master shot him a look of disbelief. "What nerve! You cost me my arms, my legs, and all of my remaining teeth and you know nothing about camels. Learn the basic rule of life. Nothing is free in this world. You get nothing for nothing."

Munna floundered helplessly. What to do? Where to go?

"Know how long it takes a date palm tree to blossom?"

Munna shook his head.

"Pay your debt first, boy. Sweat it out."

Munna's dread grew. Oh, the pressure, the tightness inside him, squeezing him like a wet rag. He recognized the pain. His curse. It had trapped him. He thought of the boys back home, sewing all day in factories, bound to their employers in exchange for a loan to their parents. They were slaves. He was a slave.

Run fool, but he couldn't. How could he?

The truck slowed around a bend in the road.

Now, he said to himself.

Munna opened his door . . . and a gust of hot wind and sand rushed in.

Master gave a shout, yanking him back with one hand, the other still on the wheel. He braked sharply. The van swerved off the road into a sandbank and stopped with a jolt. Munna tried to free himself from the man's grip, but it held. The old man was strong.

"*Bewakoof!* Stupid! You'd have killed us both." Master was breathing hard. "*Bhains ki aulad*, offspring of a buffalo! Don't ever try that again!"

Munna's chin thrust up. "Don't insult my father."

"Listen, little fighter, listen well. You're a firecracker like me, too hot for your own good. Life will be much easier if you do what I ask you to do."

Munna scowled. He would not be the man's slave. Never. The crab-hand still gripped his arm, as the man mopped his wet forehead with his other sleeve, and yanked off his glasses.

Munna stared back defiantly.

"That was a reckless move, boy. If you died, both of us would lose—you, your life, I, the help. I took you because your uncle pleaded that your family was in desperate need of money. I know what it's like to be poor. I've roamed in the gutters of India." He licked his chapped lips. "Show me your worth and I might be tempted to give you an allowance. Trust me, I'm a fair man."

Trust this creep? thought Munna. Never. "I can't—" he bit his paper-dry lip, "live here," he finished.

The grip relaxed. "A few days will ripen you." The chapped lips coiled into a blistered smile. "Trust me. Old as I am, I know a thing or two. Things happen for a reason, and in the end we learn something valuable." He raised his hands in gratitude. "The desert will grow on you. The fair maiden will thicken your hide. Make new bones. Make a man of you."

Munna sat up. He *was* the man of his house. He did not care a crow's feather about the desert teaching him. He had left home to secure his family's future and honor. He could not afford to waste a single day without pay.

"If you don't pay me I'll . . ."

"Run away," Master finished the sentence. "Run where to, eh?" He chuckled like a young boy. "Grow up, boy. Believe me, time doesn't just add wrinkles, it makes the skin thicker. Like a rhino's hide. You remind me of my caterpillar days when I was brash and green like you. See what it cost me?" He tapped his scalded face.

Ugh! God forbid, Munna thought, he didn't want an ugly frog's skin like Master's. He'd kill himself if that ever happened. But his fate was in the hands of this creep with a dagger.

He'd fake friendly, be like the clever fox who outsmarted the crow by flattery—the crow who had the bread in its mouth until it cawed.

"I'm sorry, Master-ji. I'll give it a try," Munna said.

"Am I to believe this sudden change?"

Munna nodded. "I'll do my best to help you."

Master smiled. He patted Munna's knee. "I've got big plans for you, son. I want you to head the Sheikh's ousbah. So saddle up, do as I say, and you'll be well fed and happy."

Master took control of the steering wheel, humming an old Hindi song, and began to drive.

At the Ousbah

The clunker of a truck spat and sputtered on the dusty
desolate road that cut through the heart of the desert.

"Of all the ousbahs that His Highness Sheikh Ahmed
owns, ours is the best," said Master.

Munna forced himself to smile, but remained alert for
any road signs in case he had to escape. There was nothing to see. No houses. No people. Not a cow, chick, or crow.
Miles and miles of sand, pale as a dry bone, stretching on
and on. Back home, the roads overflowed with bicycles,
buses, auto-rickshaws, and people. Ahead of them all of a
sudden, a spectacular glimmer of blue appeared.

"Lake, a lake," Munna blurted out with relief.

Master chuckled. "The gods are tricky. It's a mirage."

Munna knew what a mirage was, but he had never seen
one before. He was seeing an image of the blue sky on the
road.

The road narrowed, twisting and coiling like a sand
snake. Munna wondered if the clunker could squeeze
through. Around a bend, they turned into an area fenced by
metal topped with barbed wire that glinted in the sun. His
grip on his knapsack tightened.

They pulled up in front of a lone adobe house surrounded
by the thorny scrubland. The sun lit up the cacti and other

glossy succulents, fully erect in all their glory without inhibition. Master gave a twisted smile. "Welcome to the ousbah."

They climbed out of the truck. Munna slung his knapsack on his shoulder and followed Master down a flagstone path through the scrubland. Thorns and thistles stuck to his pants. It was eerily quiet and then suddenly they heard the sound of giggling, and they looked around. Brown young faces peeked out of the foliage, while one kid hung upside down from a branch of a small tree, like a monkey. Master raised his stick to threaten, swearing in Hindi.

An icky smell hit them as they approached an outhouse, its roof chewed up with gaping holes. "Toilet," said Master. He made a face in disgust. "The brats have stunk it up."

His stick swung south to point to a wooden shelter as long as a ship, adrift in the scrubland. "The stable for the Sheikh's camels," he said. "And next to the stable is your palace. *Tera mahel*," he smirked. "To be shared with the camel trainers."

Munna looked at the little shed attached to one end of the stable; it was typical of the alley dwellings at home, where shanties were built leaning on any surface for support. So much for his dream of living in a palace.

"Time for geography," said Master. "We are in the Empty Quarter, the Rub'al-Khalil, one of the largest sand seas on the earth." His cracked lips turned into a smile. "God guards the ousbah." He swung the stick to his left. "Hundreds of miles this way will take you to the Persian Gulf." He swung the stick to his right. "Hundreds of miles that way will take you to the Gulf of Oman."

Munna's heart sank; he clenched his fists inside his pocket. He couldn't swim, but even if he could, he'd never make it anywhere.

The stick pointed toward the rows of rolling dunes in the

distance. "Home of djinns and sinking sands," said Master. "Remember, the more you struggle, the faster you sink. That is the law of the sand."

Already Munna felt his legs wobble.

The stick waved around. "Al-Hajar, Mountains of Doom," said Master. "Knowing your itch for daring, I warn you, don't wander. You will be lost forever. Your flesh will dry up and fall off. And watch out for the scorpions—the Deathstalker eats her own babies."

Munna had melted into a puddle of sweat, but he kept a nonchalant face. He would not give the man the satisfaction of seeing him frightened.

"Of course, you can't fly anywhere without this." Master patted his breast pocket, where Munna's passport partly stuck out. "Questions?"

Munna stood speechless.

"Don't fret, helper. God helps those who work hard," Master said, pressing his scarred hand over his chest to show God's will. The stick prodded hard at Munna's rib-cage. "Unload the truck. Cans and fodder go in the store room in the stable." He turned around and left.

Munna trudged towards the stable flanked by mighty date palms, the fruit high up beyond reach. He tried the weathered door of the shed next to the stable. It creaked, yielding to a warm cavelike space. The room was empty except for a few straw pallets and threadbare blankets on the earthen floor. A small peekaboo window let in some sun. Dumping his knapsack in a corner, Munna looked around. No light. No water. He would have to use the stinky toilet outside. Depressed, he stood rooted for a few seconds, as if caught in a bad dream. Soon he would wake up and none of this would be true.

Groping against the wall, he found and opened the

connecting door. Cool air with the stink of dung rushed through to greet him. He was in the stable. Fluorescent electric lights lit up the expansive space. Ceiling fans whirred overhead and a generator hummed. A fat fridge stood next to four large storage bins. Dragging out a step stool, he stood on it and peeked inside the bins—wheat, barley, oats, and alfalfa. Towards the middle of the stable, the walls were lined with shelves holding bottles of powders and pills and equipment like saddles, a toolbox, brushes, and cleaning supplies. Tin pails hung on hooks on the opposite wall, and standing upright in a corner were various implements: mop, broom, scoop-shovel, wheelbarrow. The end section of the stable was divided into spacious camel pens filled with hay. Each pen was three times the size of his flat back home. Lucky camels, they lived like kings. Two long troughs ran along the length of the stable, one held grain, the other, water.

He heard a gurgling sound.

"Whoa!" He gave a startled cry and spun around, falling on his rear on the hay-covered floor. A white beast as tall as a hill with googly eyes and foaming mouth stood just inches away from him. Of course, he had seen camels before, but they were brown, and he had never come so close to one before.

Quickly he rose to his feet. His eyes fixed on the white beast, he retreated, step by step, towards the far side of the pen until he reached a gate, which opened into the scrubland outside. Then he spun around and ran as far away from the beast as he could. Dear God, how would he tend to these humpy beasts?

Slowly, he fumbled his way back to Master's truck. If only he knew how to drive, he'd scram. He emptied the trunk, carrying the crates of fodder to the stable storeroom, watching out for camels. After five trips, he sat down outside for a breather. Lines of sweat ran down his face and neck. The sun had liquefied him.

His gaze roamed over the endless expanse of bare, naked land. All lay still as dead, the deep silence stretched as taut as the barbed wire on the metal fence enclosing the ousbah. The fence had been constructed from the flattened sides of oil drums. He felt lost in this vastness, trapped in an infinite sandbox. Where was he? The world he knew had vanished. Stopped spinning. Mr Joseph, his science teacher, once said that if the earth suddenly stopped rotating, the world would become hell, since the atmosphere would still be in motion and everything, including people and animals would be swept off into space.

He was in hell all right. Dead-still hell, where it was quiet, so quiet that all he heard was his breath and the taunting curse: *Loser, loser, loser.*

The curse had won; it had bewitched him to follow its deceptively wondrous scent all the way to Arabia, then gleefully clutched him in its claws. It had sucked his blood, devoured his guts, and dug a deep hole into which he had fallen.

Why had he trusted Uncle? He clutched a fistful of sand. The hot grains slipped between his fingers. Just as for Didi, his dreams, trust, hope were all gone. He had nothing to hold on to. Grabbing fistfuls of sand, he chucked them against the stable wall, again and again, sending puffs of dust flying into the air like smoke. Exhausted, he fell with his face in the sand and let out a piteous cry.

A realization suddenly dawned on his mind: if he had got into this sandpit, he could get out of it. What he needed was smarts not foolish bravado. He made up an escape plan in his mind: 1. Get his passport back from Master. 2. Escape to

Deeba. 3. Find a job to make enough money for his sisters' wedding and a ticket home.

He stood up and shambled back to the shed. He dug out his shawl from his knapsack, covered himself with it, curled into a tight ball, and shut his eyes.

The Camel Trainers

Munna sat up on the pallet, scratching an itchy ear, and saw himself staring at two chocolate faces grinning like gremlins with perfect square teeth. Crouched on his hams on the earthen floor, a baby-faced boy with bulging fish eyes squinted at him, while the other, with an acne-marked face, tried to hide a strand of hay behind his back. Who were these pranksters?

The events of the afternoon rushed back into Munna's mind. He was trapped as Master's slave in an ousbah in the desert. He must have zonked out in the tool shed. Golden streams of the evening sun splintered through the dusty porthole window. His gaze returned to the dark boys who were now holding hands. Like Master, they wore white *kurta-pyjamas*, and locks of black corkscrew curls sneaked out under their white skull caps.

"*Salam*," said the boys, one voice squeaky, the other high-pitched.

Munna shook his head. "English," he said, "I'm Munna, from India." He smiled and hoped he could glean some information from them.

"Bismillah, in the name of Allah," said the acne-faced boy in a deep guttural voice. "I, Amin. Best camel trainer from Sudan." He thumped his chest then nudged his friend, who squeaked, "I, Omer, from Sudan," and thumped his chest as well.

Sudan was in Africa! How did they end up here?

"Brothers?" Munna asked.

Amin and Omer swapped glances at each other. "Same-same," they said simultaneously, like marionettes pulled by an unseen puppeteer.

Amin said that a spirit had flown them here, and Omer added that they were searching for a milk lake under the earth.

Munna nodded, though he barely understood them.

"Your home and your families?" he asked.

"We likes to be together," they said simultaneously.

To Munna's astonishment they locked themselves into a tangled embrace, falling over each other, giggling *kit-kit-kit* like chirping crickets. Omer stood up and strutted about, wiggling his narrow hips. Munna smiled. Then Amin gestured with his hands that it was time to eat. Munna followed them to Master's house through the back door.

Inside, a creaky fan whirred overhead, a welcoming relief. Munna's gaze roamed around the room, scrutinizing every conceivable spot for his passport, but the place mirrored the barren desert, it was devoid of furniture or photographs, mirrors or curtains.

Master sat on a cushion on the floor among a pile of rocks of every color and shape. On his lap sat the fattest cat in the world, as fair as the sand outside. He pointed to the kitchen and waved the other two boys away, as if swatting at pesky flies. He smiled, patted the floor near him for Munna to sit down next to him.

"I'm a rock hound," he said gleefully. "Rocks tell us amazing stories." He went through his rock trophies: "Agate, quartz, geode, garnet, mica, iron pyrite or fool's gold, I got them all. Been working with rocks all my life. They awaken the *kundalini* energy in our spine, unblock our *chakras*, help us deal with anger, guilt, shame. Hopefully, they'll heal my wounds." His eyes shut as if in a prayer.

He opened his eyes and cradled a red rock in his palm. "Check this love rock. The Desert Rose will charge you up like a battery," he said, breaking into his good-natured smile.

Munna held the rock. Nothing. The fat cat hissed at him, ears raised like radars. The rock had charged the cat instead. He resolved to stay out of the cat's way.

"Easy, Tiger." Master rubbed the cat's belly and it purred affectionately. He placed the creature on his shoulder, holding it with his scarred hand while petting with his other. "Don't you like my helper, huh?" He put the cat down, rose, and snapped his fingers.

At once, the boys ran to Master. "Yes Master-ji," they said, standing ramrod-straight like soldiers at attention, their arms dangling at the sides of their white tunics.

"Do you see my helper," said Master, bringing their heads closer as if to knock some sense into them. "He is the leader of this ousbah," said Master.

"Yes Master-ji," said the trainers, but Munna caught the grimace on Amin's face.

Master turned to Munna. "Watch these boneheads closely," he said. "They're good only with camels, *bas*. Make sure they clean up proper. See they don't start a fire and burn my house down."

Munna nodded and followed the two trainers to the kitchen. Unlike the shed, the house was wired for electricity and hooked up with running water. He sat on the kitchen floor with the trainers, who dunked thick slices of buttered bread in their hot tea. His gaze drifted to the glass door overlooking the veranda outside. Six kids with long shaggy hair sat on the floor, eating from tin bowls. They looked like the kids they had seen outside earlier.

Munna asked the trainers: "Why are the girls eating outside?"

The baby-faced Omer giggled. "Boys," he said. "Them small boys. We, big boys."

"Whose children are they? Why do they eat outside?"

Omer tried to elaborate, but Amin wrung his ear to shush him.

The meal over, Munna made sure the two boys washed the pots and cutlery and wiped the floor. When Master came to inspect the kitchen, his fat cat writhed out of his grip. Munna backed up. The spurned cat glared fiercely at him with its yellow eyes. Behind him, he heard the trainers giggling *kik-kik-kik*. Silly boys. It wasn't funny.

Master joined the laughter. "Tiger doesn't bite," he said. He scooped up the cat and buried his face into its fur. "I found the poor thing crying in the dunes. His foot was sprained. Don't worry, Tiger will get used to you, since you'll be here for a long time."

Wishful thinking, Munna thought. He would be gone soon. "Come with me." Master's scaly hand scraped Munna's elbow and nudged him down the hallway towards the front entry.

Once more, Munna scoured the area, scrutinizing every conceivable spot. Against the far side of the wall, the bookshelf was lined with an Arabic-English dictionary, the Bhagavad Gita, the Quran, and other books.

Munna wondered, why did he have the uncomfortable feeling that he was being watched?

Ah! In a hollow in the wall was a shrine, and inside it Durga Ma sat on a stool, smiling her meditative smile, her ten arms carrying weapons and the lotus flower. They had a statue just like that at home.

Munna followed Master into an enclosure curtained off with a white sheet. A wooden chest with brass studs sat in the middle, the type used to hide jewelry for safe-keeping . . . or a dead body? A tingle ran down his spine, he held his breath. Master pulled the hinged top open and dug out two sets of neatly folded white *kurta-pyjama*, a white scarf, and a pair of plastic slippers. Phew! Munna exhaled. "You'll find these comfortable in the desert," said Master. "They'll protect you from the sun, let in air, allow the sweat to evaporate and cool you."

Munna thanked Master and left, glad to be away from him and his wild sand cat.

Back in the shed, Munna put on the *kurta-pyjama* and stashed his neatly folded clothes into his knapsack. No way would he go home in this flimsy wear. He folded his scarf and tied it around his neck like a pirate's bandana.

The trainers clapped heartily to see him dressed like them. "Same-same," they cried, kissing both his cheeks.

The rejoicing was cut short by a shrill cry.

"Scorpi, scorpi," Omer pointed to a black creature that had just crawled out from under a pallet; it scuttled across the floor, whipping its tail.

Munna was used to roaches and rats. But this black thing had many legs and claws and looked truly menacing. Amin smacked Omer on the head. "Scorpion," he corrected in his guttural voice. Munna's mind echoed with Master's warning: *Deathstalker eats its own babies.*

"Help!" he screamed, his heart racing fast.

The trainers cupped their hands over their mouths, giggling deliriously.

"No scare, no scare," said Amin, grabbing a pitchfork. "Huuya!" cried Omer, and Amin stabbed the scorpion with the pitchfork several times. "Huuya!" cried Omer again, and Amin squashed the creature with the heel of his slipper. Omer held the door open and Amin pushed the dead thing out with the pitchfork.

Munna gave out a loud sigh of relief. He clasped his hands together. Master was right. The desert was dangerous. Not just the hot sun, but its critters too.

Stable Chores

Early next day, after a skimpy breakfast of tea and bread at Master's house, Munna watched the two trainers lead the camels out from the stable and order them to sit. Then the trainers hoisted six scrawny kids in over-sized t-shirts onto the camels. They were the kids with long shaggy hair that he had earlier mistaken for girls. Who were they?

At that moment, Master charged into the stable, slamming his stick against the walls, yelling, "Helper! Where are you?"

"Here, Master-ji," said Munna, floating forward in his desert-dweller's uniform.

Master beamed at him. "Did you see our prized camels? Of all the ousbahs, ours are the finest," he said.

Munna nodded, but to him the humped beasts were stinky, slobbery, and scary.

"They are true thoroughbreds," said Master. "Camel-racing is an important heritage of the Bedouins. Sheikh Bin Ahmed has invested millions into the sport." He paused, then went on, "Racing camels need exercise every day. They will run around the ousbah. The distance will double when the racing season starts." He strode into the storeroom, surprisingly fast for a man of his age. "Racing camels need energy to run," he said. "Rule one: feed the camels before you feed yourself. Today I will prepare the feed. Tomorrow, you take over. Clear?"

"Yes, Master-ji," said Munna.

"Stay three camel-lengths away from them until you finish their feed. Make sure they understand the 'get back' command before you feed them. Clear?"

"Yes, Master-ji," said Munna, though he preferred to stay as far as possible from the beasts.

Master picked up a long wooden spatula and dug into the wheat, barley, oat, and alfalfa bins in turn, shovelling scoops into the food trough. Next, he emptied six cartons of milk, six pills from the jar labelled *Vitamins*, a bottle of honey, and a handful of medicinal leaves. Finally, he stirred the gruel with the spatula.

"Rule two. Fill these pails with water and empty them into the water trough."

Munna did as instructed and returned to find Master talking to the white camel. He wondered why it didn't go out on the exercise run with the other camels.

"Come, Snow White," Master offered his blistered palm, and the camel licked it. "Rani is the Sheikh's favorite camel and the only one allowed inside his house," said Master. "She's too old for racing but very important for breeding." He swung his stick towards the pile of dung, over which a cloud of black flies buzzed. "Rule three. Muck out the dung from the stable and dump it in the dung container every day."

"Master-ji," Munna said, "I'll make sure both the stable as well as your house are clean. I will be the best helper I can be." He grabbed the broom and began to sweep to demonstrate his diligence. An idea dawned on him, but he had to keep it secret.

"Good!" said Master. "My little helper has beauty, brawn,

and brain. Good investment."

Back from Master's house after the evening meal, Munna held the pressure lamp, searching every nook and cranny of the shed for scorpions. Satisfied, he turned down the lamp and lay on the pallet next to the two trainers. The wind whistled like a kettle outside, buffeting the walls of the shed, rattling and shaking them as if attempting to force its way inside. Djinns? Master had warned him about the djinns in the dunes.

Munna went over to peek through the porthole window. A full moon went sailing across the night sky. Ghostly moonlight shone upon the crests of the dunes in the distance, making them glow. The moon didn't even have its own light, it reflected the sun—nothing was as it appeared. The desert was full of mirages. He returned to lie down.

His ears picked up a strange sound. What was it? In answer, a chilling scream cut through the silence. He sat up. The cry of a maiden trapped in the dunes? He imagined her in a blood-red sari, spinning round and round, her black hair flying. Her face ran with tears, her mouth was open. Didi, pleading for help.

It couldn't be. Didi was dead.

He shook the trainers awake. "Omer, Amin, can you hear the noise? Is it the djinns?"

Looking dazed at first, they glanced at each other, then started giggling. Amin said the desert was a trickster. Munna lay back down, his heart still racing. He had to bolt from here as soon as he could.

Weighing Day

After breakfast the next morning, Master raised his stick in the air with an announcement: "Today is Weighing Day." He dismissed the trainers, and put his scalded arm around Munna's shoulder as though the two of them were besties. "Bring the scale."

Munna found the scale under the kitchen cabinet. He carried the scale outside, tagging along after the man like his loyal puppy, down the flagstone path through the backyard to a small tin shack partially hidden by long grass. As they stood outside Master yelled some command, and to Munna's surprise the six scrawny kids he had seen before jostled out on their stick legs like baby chicks. Kids they were, but their crusty crinkled faces made them look more like dwarves.

"Camel boys," said Master. "From Bangladesh, Pakistan, and Afghanistan." Munna refrained from asking whose kids they were and who had brought them here. Who looked after them? "They speak and understand simple English." Master twirled his stick like a tiger-tamer at a circus. In response, the boys huddled closer to each other as though protecting themselves.

"Do you see my helper?" Master yelled. "He's your leader. You must obey him."

"Yes, Master-ji," murmured the boys, staring at Munna in spiteful silence. Munna shifted his weight from one foot to the other. The stares shifted to the scale in his hands; they looked at it fearfully, as though it were a loaded gun. Munna put it down by his feet.

"Let's go through the rules for camel jockeys," said Master. He began to pronounce them one by one.

"No fighting unless you like a thwacking." Master swung his stick in the air.

"Yes, Master-ji," murmured the boys.

"No crying for your Ma," yelled Master. He eyed the littlest boy, who had a scar across his gaunt cheek. He looked like a toddler who had just learned to walk.

"Ha-ji, Master-ji," whispered the boys.

Master turned to Munna. "Bring unruly *junglees* to my attention." He whipped his stick in the air with a whir. "A few licks will smarten them up." He commanded, "Get in a line. Step on the scale, one at a time." He looked at Munna. "Weigh them every week. Over forty pounds must be punished."

Munna nodded, though he didn't quite understand.

The first boy, likely the oldest, stepped on the scale. He had a fine aquiline nose and piercing green eyes.

"Akber's our best jockey, but at twelve, he's getting too old," said Master.

One by one, the boys stepped on the scale and Master read their weight. One boy, with a prominent overbite, hit exactly forty-two pounds on the scale. "Make sure he loses five pounds," said Master. "Extra runs with weights tied to his feet should do it."

Munna nodded.

"You." Master poked his stick at the littlest one, who gave a squeal. "This brat is trouble."

The boy stuck his tongue out, but thankfully Master didn't see it. The boy stepped on the scale. Twenty-six pounds. Munna gasped.

The last boy stood on the scale uncertainly, sucking a finger in his mouth. "My chikoo," said Master, pinching the boy's cheeks fondly.

Of course, Master liked meek lambs.

The stick prodded Munna's shoulder. "Fail to discipline them, and I will discipline you."

Master dismissed the boys, and they fled like chickens from a fox.

"Master-ji," Munna blurted. "Why do we need to keep their weight down?"

"Short answer: do as you are told. Long answer: The lighter the kids, the faster the camels can run. And the faster the camels run, the more chances to win the race, no?" So saying, he spun around, picked up the scale, and left.

Munna was bothered. It was wrong to make little boys work, wrong to starve them, wrong to punish them. As Master's helper, he was an accomplice, his partner-in-crime. He felt a lump in his throat. *Run*, urged the voice inside him. Run away from the starving boys, run away from the oppressive silence of the desert, run away from the camels. But run where? Back home, when his curse oppressed him, he'd run to his hidey-hole under the bottom stairs of his building, but where could he hide here? The sea of sand stretched on as far as he could see, while his muddled mind was a forest of raging wild, animals. He was lost.

Later, inside the kitchen at Master's house, Amin and Omer placed six tin bowls on a cardboard tray, filling half of each with *daal* and half with water, and six crusty buns, which they carried to the camel boys on the veranda outside. When they returned, Munna sat with them on the tiled kitchen floor to eat. Master had given them a bowl of rice and a simmering pot of vegetable curry sprinkled with coriander leaves. Munna was impressed that Master had cooked. The curry tasted delicious.

"Big boys eat good food," said Omer.

Munna dug into the curry and rice. Through the glass door overlooking the veranda outside, he saw the camel boys: Akber, Ajit, Smiley, Mustapha, Babur, and Shanti. They ripped their bread into pieces and dipped them into the watery *daal*, and gobbled them up. Starved to keep down their weight down, this was their only meal after the skimpy breakfast.

Munna felt sick. Back in Guj, he had seen street boys paw through rubbish heaps, but he didn't know them. Knowing the camel boys intensified his anguish, the guilt rising to his mouth in a bitter taste. Every bit of food was hard to swallow. He gulped a glass of water to wash the food down. He pushed aside his plate, which still had rice on it, and dashed out of the house into the backyard. He hit the grass feeling nauseous. He lay on his side to let the sickness pass. But it only grew. He retched, clutching his belly, tried to throw up. Nothing would come up. Finally, he pushed two fingers into his mouth and with a spasm threw out everything he had eaten. Out poured the shame and disgust.

Babur

The same routine followed the next day. After a skimpy breakfast of tea and bread at Master's house, the trainers left with the boys strapped on their camels for their daily exercise. Munna cleaned the stable, forking the dung out from the camel pens and tossing it into its container. He heard a noise outside.

He opened the door a crack and peeked outside. Master sat on the bench that was there, eating dates from a bowl. At his feet sat one of the camel boys, one of the smaller ones, his hands tied behind his back. Master amused himself, spitting the pits at a farther distance each time. The fun over, he rose, whipped out his dagger from under his tunic, and cut the rope from the boy's hands.

The boy grabbed Master's forearm and bit into it. Master pulled his arm back, foaming at the mouth. Revenge was fast and furious. Master slapped the boy's cheek, swearing a spate of oaths while the boy raised his chicken-wing arm to protect himself.

Master pulled the boy's frayed shorts down, pushing his head down to the ground. "Down, *kuta!* Dog!"

Munna flinched at the thwack of Master's stick on the boy's backside, followed by a thin cry. How could he stop the beating? He looked around the stable, the cries of the boy tearing at him. The white camel lay asleep, its legs folded and tucked under its body. Slowly, Munna crept up to the far side of the pen and unlatched the gate there. Then he found a broom and poked it at the camel's flank.

"Wake up lazy bum! Go, eat grass," he whispered.

The camel stood up, and Munna sprang away from its path just in time as it bolted through the open gate. Hearing the beat of camel hooves, Master looked up. He swore an oath, straightened himself, and started to chase the runaway, his arms flailing.

"Rani, Rani!" He slipped and fell flat on the sand.

God is great. Munna gave a helping hand to Master, who sat up, wiping his dusty face against the sleeve of his tunic. "Did you touch Rani?" he asked.

"I . . . I was . . . sweeping the pen . . ." Munna stammered.

"Foolish boy! A camel's kick can kill you! Didn't I tell you Rani is the Sheikh's favorite camel?" He peered in the direction where the camel had run. "I'll get her." He gave his stick to Munna. "Strike the brat until he repents," he said and left.

Munna glanced at the boy, who hitched up his frayed shorts, but they fell right back. His eyes were too big for his face, his face was too big for his scrawny self, and his hair was too long. A scar ran from his brow to his gaunt cheek like a zipper.

The boy stared at the stick, his nose running.

Munna threw down the stick. "I won't hurt you," he said softly.

The boy drew closer, slowly. Aw! He stank.

"I, good boy," he said, lisping through his missing teeth.

Munna smiled. He could see himself in the little boy. "I'm sure you are." He wiped the gaunt cheek with his scarf, but the grime held. The boy gazed up at him in admiration with his big brown eyes, as if he were the most wonderful person in the world.

"My bhaiya," the boy said in an endearing voice.

"No, I am not your brother," Munna said. "I'm your friend, okay?"

"You too biiig to be my friend."

"I'm Master's helper," Munna said. But he had risked Master's wrath by saving the boy. "I may not be able to save you again."

"I brave boy," said the boy fiercely.

Munna smiled. "What's your name?"

"Babur."

"How did you come here, Babur?"

"I dunno."

"How old are you, Babur?"

"Dunno," said the boy. He caught Munna's arm, his face scrunched up to cry. "I don't wants to die."

"You will not die," Munna said. He tried to pull free but the boy's grip tightened.

"I scared. When camels run *ba boom, ba boom*, Sajid fall and the camel crush him."

Munna was afraid of camels too. He didn't know what to say. He couldn't risk his neck for the boy, he had to spare himself for his family.

"You are a brave boy, Babur, but you must stay out of trouble," he said.

"I no trouble." The thick dark brows knitted together into one. "I good boy."

"Good boys do what they're told. Good boys obey Masters," said Munna.

The boy shook his head vigorously. "When I be biiig and strong like you, I kill all Masters and camels." He pointed his two bony fingers and went: "*Bang-bang-bang.*"

Munna held the boy's tiny fingers. "Good boys don't do that."

Finally, Munna pulled away from the clinging boy. "I'm busy," he said, and walked back towards the shed.

"I likes you, Bhaiya," the boy said after him, and ran away.

Later, when Munna went to the house for the evening meal, Master was waiting for him.

"Thank the stars, Rani's fine. She belongs to the distinctive Omani breed of camels. Do you know how much the Sheikh paid for her?"

Munna shook his head.

"Ten million dhirams," said Master. Munna didn't know how many rupees that was, but it seemed like a lot of money. "One foolish mistake and both you and I will be the Sheikh's *daal*. Didn't you milk cows and look after chickens?"

"I went to school," said Munna, raising his chin. He wasn't the typical Indian village boy who raised cows and chicken. Ma and his sisters had worked hard to keep him in school.

"Well, Smarty, don't foul up your nest," said Master. He strode over to the bookshelf against the far side of the wall, picked out a black book as thick as a dictionary and tossed it to Munna. "Put your schooling to use. Read all about camels before you attempt to touch one."

Munna read the title: *The Camel Book*. He didn't care a bit about those beasts. He wanted to rip the pages of the book and shove them down the man's throat.

Master raised two knotty fingers. "Either be my dung boy or a responsible helper."

Munna had a third option, but that was a secret. He put

on his game face and said, "Master-ji, I'll chew every word in this book. I will not disappoint you."

"Good," said Master.

Back after the evening meal, Munna lay on the pallet in the shed, trying to read *The Camel Book* in the dim light. Next to him, the trainers curled up like twin spoons on the pallet, their rumbling snores rising and falling. Babur had captured Munna's mind. The little boy reminded Munna of his own younger days . . . When the first rains fell, he'd peel his clothes off, run outside, let the cold rain pelt his chest. He would slosh his bare feet in the rain puddles. In a few days, the birds sang, the bugs crick-cricked, the streams swelled up.

But there was one spooky monsoon night when he and his family waited anxiously for their father to come home from the rock quarry where he worked. Didi hoisted Munna at the window to show him the roaring rain. It rained so hard that water gushed into their apartment like a waterfall. Ma and his sisters were mopping up the mess when a djinn with donkey legs and goat horns broke into their flat, shaking a beer bottle in his hand. Water dripped off its head and hairy chest, its eyes were red as blood, dancing unsteadily, and in a slurring voice he yelled for Ma's purse. Ma fell to her knees, but the djinn threw the beer bottle at her. Luckily it hit the wall, glass flying everywhere. Munna had been so scared, he had wet his pants. Later when he was older, Didi told him that the djinn he thought he had seen was really their rain-drenched father . . .

Munna slammed the book shut and the trainers woke up with a start. Amin sat up and gazed suspiciously at the darkness. The frightened Omer pulled his blanket over himself, sniffling, while the brave Amin went to check at the door, and then yelled, "Bismillah," and punched his fist at his own shadow on the wall. He duly announced: "You's safe." Munna returned to his thoughts about Babur. The little boy was alone; he had no one in his life to look up to. It felt good to be Babur's brother even if he really wasn't.

The Camel Boys

The sun's first rays were kind to Munna, but only for a couple of hours, after which it unleashed all its fury. He hurried to finish his stable chores and then walked over to check on Babur. The boys' shanty was hidden by long grass and thorny scrub. When he arrived outside, he heard screaming and shouting. He rapped on the tin door several times. Getting no answer, he pushed it open.

He entered a dark cave stinking of urine. He stumbled onto an empty can and kicked it out of his way. As his eyes adjusted to the darkness, the images around him took shape. Two boys were trying to push each other against the wall, others egging them on. The dirt floor was littered with cans, crates, hay, dry leaves, and newspaper scraps, the aftermath of a throwing match. He coughed. There were no windows. Tiny holes punched in the tin walls let in air with the dust.

Babur ran to Munna, pressing his head against his arm endearingly: "My Bhaiya."

Munna ruffled the boy's hair, a tangled mess. As his gaze roamed over other gritty faces, it was apparent that they all begged for a good scrub-down. Didi would have scoured them until their skins shone.

The handsome, green-eyed boy glared at Munna. "Hey Big Boy, what do you want?" Master had said that he was their best jockey, but too old at twelve. He raised his fist, flexing his puny biceps at Munna. "I can fight you, Big Boy."

"I'm your friend," said Munna, alarmed. "I came to help you."

"Liar," said the boy. "Go home, Big Boy."

The boy with the overbite said, "I, Mustapha . . ." Before he could finish, the handsome boy pounced on him, twisting his arm. "Scorpion, I'll break your neck."

"Aw, aw, aw," cried Mustapha. "Let go, Akber."

The piercing green eyes sought Munna's. "I'm Akber the Great," he said.

"Then you better behave like one," said Munna. "C'mon boys, the party's over, it's clean-up time. Let's build a tower." He began to pick the discarded litter and piled it into the corner. Babur topped the pile with cans while the others looked on.

Akber kicked at the tower. The cans toppled onto the mud floor. "Big Boy is Monster-ji's new pet," he told the boys.

"I'm not," said Munna. He wanted to say that he too hated Master and he sympathized with them. But he kept quiet.

"I for you, Bhaiya," Babur said. Mustapha shrugged, unsure of his alliance, while the others edged near Akber, acknowledging him as their leader. Lost momentarily in his thoughts, Munna came to himself and dug out a few marbles from his pockets. He rolled them in his palm, watching the shiny eyes staring at them. He pitched a few marbles into the air with one hand and caught them with his other hand, then he raised a leg and threw them under, catching them as they arched over his head. The boys whooped in amazement.

"C'mon, let's see who can shoot the farthest!" Munna said.

"Me, me," cried the boys in excitement, shoving each other to come forward.

They clustered around Munna. He got onto his knees, bent his forefinger, and showed them how to flick and shoot a marble. Each boy got a turn. When it was Akber's turn, he spat on the ground. "I don't play baby games," he said. Munna ignored him and pocketed his marbles. He told the boys he had come all the way from India and that he missed his Ma and his sisters. "Tell me about your families."

"Me," cried Babur. "My Ma's eyes are . . ." he tilted his head skywards. "Blue," he finished.

"Liar!" Akber shouted. "You always make up stories."

"I dunno. I forgot," Babur squeaked in a tiny voice. Munna pulled Babur close to him. "Babur's too young to remember his Ma," he said.

"Then he ought to shut up," said Akber, glaring at Babur.

"I, I," said Mustapha. "My father be a farmer in Cholistan. My Kaka-ji takes me to buy a new bike but drops me here seven tooths ago." He dug out from his pocket seven fallen teeth and held them in his pale pink palm. They marked his time at the ousbah.

Munna glanced at Akber to indicate it was his turn to speak, but Akber bugged his eyes, flapped his ears, and stuck his tongue out. The boys all laughed.

Once again, the eager Mustapha blurted: "We be cousins. Akber's new step-ma kick him out of the house." He rose up to demonstrate the kick.

"I'm sorry," Munna told Akber.

"She's a witch and a bitch," said Akber.

Munna glanced at the next boy.

"Ajit," he said, but everyone laughed, chanting, "Susu!" implying that he was a bed-wetter.

"Go on, Ajit," said Munna. Embarrassed, the boy covered his eyes with his hands and said, "My sick Ma cough so much blood, so Aunty-ji brings me here to make my Ma good."

Munna nodded. He looked at the next boy, who had deep dimples.

"Smiley," said the boy, holding both palms up. "I gets five brothers and five sisters; but no *roti*. My Bapu say I lucky to be jockey."

Munna's gaze flew to the last boy, Master's "chikoo." Slumped in the corner, he was staring at his curled toes.

"He is Shanti. He don't talk," said Mustapha.

"How are you, Shanti?" said Munna.

Shanti raised his gaze a little, his eyes soulless and flat.

Munna yearned to comfort him, but how? He looked at the boys. "God will bless all of you," he said, sounding much like his Ma.

"I don't wants blesses," whined Babur. "I wants my Ma."

"Shut up!" Akber rose to his knees. "Your Ma don't want you," he said. "Nobody wants us. We are d-e-a-d. We are *bhoot bacha*, ghost boys," he sang in an eerie keening tenor, and the other boys joined in to make a pathetic chorus.

Munna scrambled to his feet and left hastily.

Back in his shed, he sat on the pallet, picked up *The Camel Book*. Camels were said to be the gods of the desert. *Camels carry the heaviest of loads with little sustenance.* Suddenly, he smacked his forehead and broke into hysterical laughter. Stupid, stupid, he was so stupid. He'd escape on a camel. All he had to do was learn to ride!

Learning to Ride

Munna woke up at dawn in absolute stillness, no wind, no creatures. Outside, a deep shade of eggplant-purple slanted across the sky. He worked hard and fast at his stable chores and was done before noon. There was no sight of Amin and Omer. He looked everywhere, and finally he discovered them in a dark corner of the stable, playing shadow detectives with a flashlight, its beams dancing on a wall.

"Can you please teach me to ride a camel?" Munna asked.

They eyed each other uncertainly. "You's Big Boy," said Omer, "camel boys ride camels." Amin's eyes narrowed, as he added, "Master-ji don't say to teach you."

"I want to surprise Master," said Munna.

"Not now, Friend. It's show time," said Amin, focusing the flashlight on Munna's face. Standing sideways, Amin pressed his hands together to cast a shadow animal on the wall. As he bent his fingers, the shadow looked like the jaws of an animal. Amin moved a finger slightly to make an eye and crossed his thumbs, pointing them up for ears. "Guess," he said.

"Fox," said Munna.

"Master-ji's cat," said Omer, and Amin clapped his hands heartily, saying, "Clever Omer." Linking his hands, his

71

fingers moving, he cast a long shadow on the wall. "Who's that?" he asked.

"Scorpion?" said Munna.

"Wrong!" said Amin gleefully, looking at his clever friend Omer.

Munna shrugged. The trainers were taking absolute delight in proving him wrong. "Okay, showtime's over," he said, "It's riding time."

Amin shook his head. "Is not a nice day to ride, friend," he said.

Munna decided against insisting too much. The trainers, fond of stirring trouble, could snitch on him to Master about his sudden interest in riding.

He'd learn by observing. At feed time, he watched the camels dip their long necks into the food trough and start chewing. Later, he saw them fold their legs and lie down. He sat beside them on the hay-lined floor, flipping through *The Camel Book. The camel must recognize you. Take your time and develop a good trusting relationship. Make the camel familiar with your smell, your voice, and your presence.*

What camel would he bond with?

Shenu was shy and quiet. He would be safe with her. He stole into Shenu's pen, gaping at the gangly camel, not sure what to do next.

"Sit," he said, but the camel stared at him with googly eyes. "Sit," he said again. But when the camel came closer, he shrieked and shot out of the stable.

The trainers saw him and laughed their heads off.

Determined to take over the reigns of leadership, Munna awoke the trainers before sun-up. He threw a pitchfork to Amin and a shovel to Omer and told them to clean the stable. The stable chores finished two hours earlier, giving Munna time to attend to his plan. He paid another visit to Shenu to try again to establish a relationship of trust between them.

The camel lay limply on her side, in her pen, fast asleep. "You are just a giant cow with a hump, right?" Munna said.

The camel didn't stir.

Munna sat on the floor of the camel pen and read *The Camel Book* aloud. Tired, he bared his heart to the camel, telling her about his secret dream of fame, about Ma and his sisters, and his plan to escape from here. He had called it My Great Escape. It felt good to empty his heart. As a final gesture, he tied his scarf loosely around his neck and danced and sang like his favorite actor, Salman Khan.

The camel stirred. She sat up and cocked her head, her ears flicking back and forth as though to the rhythm of his Hindi song and almost smiling. Did she like him or the song? He pledged to court the shy Shenu until he won her over.

Next morning Munna was mucking out the camel pens when he saw Master's truck drive away. Good. He threw aside his pitchfork and ran to the trainers, who were singing and scrubbing the camels outside the stable. Once more, he asked them to teach him to ride.

Amin eyed Omer, who looked up into the cloudless sky and frowned. He turned to Munna and said, "Sorry, friend, bad day today."

Munna knew the nice day would never come. Twelve days had gone by with hardly any progress. The wings of his game plan were wobbling; it would never fly. He sank on the stable floor, a heaviness pressing over him as if he were buried under the dunes.

The bright promise he had made to Ma might never be kept.

The Camel Ride

Days passed. Munna settled into the dusty rhythm of life at the ousbah, soaking in everything about camels as fast as a thirsty man in a desert would gulp down water. Still, he didn't dare ride a camel. And the trainers always cooked up excuses to avoid teaching him. One afternoon, when his chores were over, he decided to bait them. He called the trainers. "Amin, Omer—watch, I'll make this marble disappear."

They watched as Munna held up the marble between his index finger and thumb and covered it with his other hand to hide their view. Then he snapped his fingers, covertly letting the marble slip into his sleeve. "Voilà!" he cried, opening his fingers one by one to show his empty hands.

"You's good! You's good!" the two boys cried out in admiration.

"How you do?" asked the sly Amin.

"Ah, now." Munna had pinned them. "I can show you after you teach me to ride," he said.

The trainers looked at each other for approval. Amin spoke in Arabic to Omer, who covered his mouth with his hand as if to hide a smile. Then Amin turned to Munna and said, "Friend, today good day to ride."

They left for the stable and returned, leading the lazy white camel by a rope.

"Rani slow. Slow good for learners," said Amin.

Munna preferred Shenu, but he complied. After all, the trainers had broken every camel on the ousbah and knew better than him. The last thing he wanted was a kick from an unruly camel.

"*Kush*," Omer hissed at the camel from the back of his teeth and it duly sank down on the sand. Amin placed the saddle on the camel. "Sit," he said to Munna. Munna drew closer, but the beast opened its jaws wide, yellow teeth long and sharp as scythes. One snap of the jaw and those scythes would stab his neck, sever his jugular vein. He backed away very quickly. The trainers cupped their hands upon their mouths, delirious with laughter. Munna was hot with embarrassment.

"No scare." Omer stroked the seated camel's flank. "See."

Munna stroked the camel's flank cautiously and Omer's laughter broke through again. Amin wrung Omer's ear, chiding him in Arabic, then turned to Munna. "Sit," he said, patting the saddle. "Sit, sit. No scare."

Omer held the reins. Munna carefully placed one foot in the stirrup and swung his other leg over, scrambling to hitch up on the saddle. He tried to catch the rope from the halter around the camel's head, when Amir slapped its rump and cried out, "Bismillah!"

The camel rose on its rear legs, still kneeling on its front legs, pitching Munna forward into a precarious face-down position. He held on to the saddle for dear life, afraid to breathe, afraid he'd fly over the camel's head and crash to the ground. Before he could get his breath back, the camel rose suddenly on its front legs.

"Get me down," Munna cried.

"Huyah! Huyah!" Amin shouted, whacking the camel's hind legs with a twig.

The camel broke into a jerking motion forward, swaying front to back and side to side.

"Help!" cried Munna, and he lost his grip on the reins.

He bent forward to reach them, but the camel swayed alarmingly, the decorative beads on its long neck jangling. "Stop!" Munna cried, but the trainers made no effort to stop the camel. A little further up the road, the camel turned, and Munna caught a glimpse of the trainers holding onto their stomachs, laughing their silly heads off. They had tricked him. Up-down, up-down, the camel bounced him in the hot afternoon sun. Sweat ran down Munna's face, his clammy hands holding on to the saddle. How would he stop the beast? The reins dangled along the side of the saddle. If he bent a little more, he'd reach it, but what if he fell?

Finally, the camel slowed down into a trot as it approached a tall stone wall. What was behind it? Munna didn't have to wait long to find out. The camel ambled through an open gate in the wall. Beyond it was a turquoise-tiled courtyard surrounded by a garden with tall palm trees. Beyond the garden stood a big white marble palace looking like the Taj Mahal.

The camel folded its legs and Munna fell on the ground, water from a fountain spraying his face.

The brass-studded door of the palace flung open and a beautiful figure of a woman in a white gown ran towards him. Munna blinked in astonishment, staring at her, tongue-tied. She lifted her veil off her face, looking as surprised as him. She threw her arms around the camel, sang a melodious song to it in what sounded like Arabic, rubbing it behind the ears as it bellowed with affection.

He scrambled to get up. "English," he managed to say.

"You mustn't ride Rani," she said in perfect English.

"I . . . I didn't." He pointed an accusing finger at the

camel. "He brought me here."

"She," said the girl, laughing. "Rani's a *naga*, a girl. Are you new?"

He nodded dumbly.

"I am Malika," she said.

The camel nudged her head against Malika's arm. "Wait, I'll be back." She hitched up her long gown and ran inside the palace. When she returned, her hand was closed into a fist. "Honey," she offered the sugar crystals to the camel.

She stroked its bulging belly. "Rani's impregnated by the strong-boned Sudanic camels of the Anafi breeding stock. Her baby will be my pet calf. I can't wait to see her."

So Rani was expecting. No wonder she didn't go on morning runs like other camels.

The girl whispered: "You can't ride Rani in her condition. My father, the Sheikh, will be angry."

Munna gaped. She was the Sheikh's daughter. His gaze darted fearfully. How would he go back to the ousbah? A stern old lady came shuffling towards them. She cast a disapproving glance at him and chided Malika in Arabic, the language also spoken by the trainers.

Malika turned to Munna and said in a loud voice, "Thanks for bringing Rani." Still under the scrutiny of the stern lady, he nodded. Malika quickly whispered, "I'll tell the servant to walk you back with Rani to the ousbah."

He nodded again, relieved. He had learned his lesson: if you don't lead a camel, it will lead you. He would tie his camel before trusting others.

Back at the ousbah, the curious trainers ran to him, their black eyes bright with mischief. "Good ride?" Omer asked.

"Very good," he said, though his back was sore. "The Princess sends her regards to you."

The trainers stared at him in disbelief.

Munna's Revenge

Following Munna's adventure with Rani, he continued to befriend Shenu all week. One afternoon as he entered Shenu's pen, to his terror, she came trotting towards him. He stood rock-still, barely breathing, the hairs on his neck on edge. Shenu bent her head, flaring her nostrils, sniffing him all over. Then her ears pricked and she swiveled around and grunted softly.

Munna tried to pat the camel. He put out a finger to touch her back: thick and woolly. Slowly, the rest of his hand went caressing down to her face, and when it came to her cheek, she licked it. *Yes! She knew him. She knew him all right.*

The next day, he looked right into Shenu's date-dark eyes and said in a firm voice: "I'm your leader. Listen to me." Then he said, like the trainers did, "*Kush, kush!*"

She sank to the floor.

He dug out from his pocket a few sugar cubes he had stolen from Master's house and offered them to her, the way Malika had done to Rani. Shenu chomped on the treat, her head wobbling. He gave her a good rub, scratching her furry ears and gangly neck down to her shoulders and she gurgled. Delighted, all his nervousness gone, he held a pretend microphone in his hand and began to sing and dance.

She grunted softly again as if to say: *I like your dance.*

Munna had wooed Shenu over as his best friend in the ousbah. Yes! He was ready for his revenge against the tricksters. He could barely suppress his delight. All that remained was to learn more about Shenu's digestive system and experiment a little with her meals.

When Friday dawned, Munna was ready to launch his plan on the trainers. Quickly, he flipped the pages of his camel book until he came across the part that explained how the camels were purged before races. He read it once more until he was fully confident of his plan. First, he prepared the usual camel feed. Then he added some purgative pills to it and offered the intestinal cocktail to Shenu.

"Sweetie, today is all-you-can-eat day," he said.

Shenu dipped her head eagerly into the pail, crunching and chomping and grunting. "Take your sweet time," he said, and sat on the floor of the pen beside her. In about an hour, she burped and belched, stinking up the entire stable. "Good job," he said, thumping the camel's flank and she broke wind, sending him reeling back. "Whoa, Stinker! You are ripe-ready."

Next, he ran outside to look for the trainers. They were playing outside, chasing each other. "Amin, Omer, over here," he called. "I have a surprise for you."

They frolicked over to him, probably thinking he'd show them more tricks.

"Friends, I was feeding Shenu when she began to talk," said Munna. The trainers exchanged looks of disbelief. "I'm pretty sure she spoke in Arabic," said Munna.

The sly Amin drew closer to Munna, eyes searching his face.

"What she say?"

"I don't know Arabic."

Omer slapped Amin's shoulder. "Allah has ninety-nine names, but camels know the hundredth name," his voice trilled with excitement. "Let's go, brother. Let's find out." They barged into the stable straight into Shenu's pen, Munna after them. Shenu sat on the hay-lined floor, bellowing and belching. Omer reached the camel first, but Amin shoved him aside. Munna stood a yard away from them watching, waiting in anticipation.

The trainers crouched on the floor near Shenu's backside, their ears close to the camel's bloated belly. Quick as a blink, Munna slipped behind Shenu, lifted her tail, and whacked it, quickly jumping out of the way.

An outburst of gas exploded from Shenu's backside, as if she had blown her intestines clean. No other animal could have matched that stink or the noise. The screaming Amin fell back on the screaming Omer. Munna laughed so much, he was out of breath. Ha! He who laughs last, laughs the most. It was by far his best day at the ousbah.

Retrieving His Passport: The First Try

Munna flexed his legs, weary and footsore. The fiery sun had turned his feet red, puffy, and blistered. His callused soles were thick as camel hide. His life back home was but a distant dream.

Amin and Omer ran over to him. "Friend, its spa day today," they cried.

Munna had learned that the trainers would lead the camels about a mile away to the Camel Hospital where they would be oiled, massaged, and groomed. Lucky camels, he scratched his itchy arm, his dry skin cracked and peeling.

"Camels get biiig bath," Omer spread his arms wide apart.

"Pool," Amin corrected, smacking Omer on the head and they jostled playfully.

"Master-ji come too. You's alone," said Omer.

Munna made a face, but he could barely hide his delight. His hour was here. Finally.

He hung around the wash area and waved cheerfully to the trainers as they led the camels out, followed by Master in his truck. The camel boys were likely in their shack. The coast was clear.

Munna made for Master's house. The back door was open. He stepped inside cautiously, alert for Tiger. No sign of the wild creature. Good. He headed straight towards the front entry, pausing hesitantly by the shrine in the hollow of the wall, his gaze colliding with the spellbinding stare of the deity, Durga Ma, her stony eyes boring into him, getting access to his feelings, issuing a warning: *I protect this house against thieves.*

"I've only come to take what's mine," said Munna, offering a delicate smile to the Goddess.

Now if he were Master, he would lock the important stuff in a safety deposit box in the bedroom. But the room was stark empty except for the mattress, covered with a quilt of faded flowers. He checked under the pillow, under the mattress. Nothing. He flung open the cracked old wooden wardrobe, its door carved with flower motifs. Nothing, except a few clothes folded in a neat pile and a pen. Ah, the pen was attached to a compass. He pocketed it.

Reaching the rear of the house, he dropped to his knees, checking the area where Master usually sat, under old pillows and throws. Nothing. He looked inside the ragged cloth bag. Just rocks. Righting himself, he checked the kitchen, flinging open every cabinet, fumbling through the contents: spice jars, moong, lentils, rice. The pantry: ghee, soup cans, milk cans. He pulled open the drawers. Cutlery.

A scuffling. Mice? He tiptoed stealthily towards the noise, hearing the smacking of slippers on the cement floor. A shiver rolled down his back as he glimpsed Master at the front door, the cat cradled in his arms. Quickly, he tried to squeeze into the hollow in the wall by the shrine, but Master spotted him. The startled man swayed on his wobbly legs and reached out to grasp the stool on which stood the idol. It fell to the floor, taking along with it the idol. Crash! Durga Ma shattered into a million pieces.

"Master-ji, are you okay?" asked Munna.

There was no reply. Master-ji, on the floor, stared at the shards scattered across the floor, and shook his head despondently as though his world had tipped, moaning in a choked voice, the cat purring. There was no mistaking the sadness on the man's face as his gaze held the broken pieces.

Munna's mouth opened, closed, opened, again.

"It broke . . . my only memento," Master said.

He picked up a jagged piece from the floor, looked at it sadly. "Once I had everything one would wish for. My wife, a thousand petals of lotus, my four little angels, all gone . . ."

Munna bit his tongue. The poor man must have lost his family in the fire that had burned him.

"I'm sorry, Master-ji," he said.

Master snapped out of his reverie, wiped his eyes against his sleeve, picked his cat, and rose. "What are you doing here?" he asked.

"I . . . I was cleaning," he stammered.

Master's forehead scrunched. "Look, if you want your passport I will gladly hand it over to you, but trust me, crossing the desert is a ticket to hell. In any case, I don't like a cheeky lad snooping in my house. Clear? Now, *chap-chap*, clean up this mess."

"Yes Master-ji," said Munna, looking for the broom.

His Great Escape had failed miserably.

The Racing Track

Early next morning, Master drove Munna to the Al-Salaam Racing Track. The truck rattled out of the ousbah, onto a road with the sign, Paradise Vale. Munna watched the terrain passing outside the car window. Under the sun's fierce eye, a stand of thorny trees with leafless limbs stood like petrified skeletons. One spiky cactus poked out of the ground like a dead man's hand. They passed the metal fence topped with barbed wire, on to the desolate tarmac road, the aorta of the desert. Munna's eyes strained against the endless brilliant yellow everywhere he looked, and he thought of the green paddy fields outside his home-town of Guj.

"The Racing Season starts tomorrow," said Master. "You will round up the trainers and the camels with the boys on them, and walk them down to the racing track. Practice races will be held every day except Fridays and Sundays. Got to be fit if we want to win the marathon, no?"

"What about my stable chores?" said Munna.

"You've got the whole afternoon for that," said Master.

Munna wondered when he would find the time to learn riding.

Soon, they approached a sign which read, Al-Salaam Racetrack. Master parked the truck and glanced at Munna.

"Did you follow the road?"

Munna nodded. "First right after the turnoff at the ousbah onto Paradise Vale."

"Good," said Master, smiling broadly, hitting his hand on the wheel. "Your uncle was right. You're sharp, as sharp as my dagger!"

Munna felt a rush of blood warm up his cheeks. Despite what he felt about Master, he was flattered.

"And will you find your way here in the dark?"

Munna nodded.

They got out of the truck and entered the racing track. The stadium was huge, and looked like a white tent, with a rolling carpet of lush green grass going around it. The lawn was watered by underground sprinklers and edged with bright cactus blossoms—yellow, pink, and orange. Inside, the grandstand was filled with tiered rows of stuffed chairs, each with a monitor. On the opposite side was raised a big white screen.

Master swung his stick to make a point. "The racing track is two concentric circles. The outer track is for Masters with trucks that chase the camel jockeys, who ride on the inner track."

Munna nodded. The outer track was tarmac, the inner, sandy; the two tracks coiled around each other like black and white serpents. Presently they heard a thunder of hooves, followed by shadows dancing along the sun-scorched inner track. A train of camels, their tiny riders strapped on their backs like dolls, came galloping along.

"From another ousbah," explained Master.

Munna nodded and wondered, how many ousbahs and camel boys were there?

"I'll meet you at the Start Gate tomorrow at four," said Master.

Munna frowned. Did he hear right? "Four in the morning?" he asked.

"That's what I said."

Munna followed Master's impatient footsteps back to his van, wondering how he would get up so early.

"Questions?" Master asked as they drove off.

Munna had plenty. "Master-ji, why are the jockeys children?"

"Is there anything lighter than boys that can control camels?" replied Master.

Munna shook his head. "But . . . but . . ."

"Not your or my business," snapped Master. "The Sheikh is my boss, I follow his orders. I am your boss, you follow mine. Chewing more *roti* than you can ingest will choke you."

Silence reigned for a few strained moments, before Master broke it. "The poverty-stricken parents of those boys are more than happy to earn a tidy sum. Their loss is a sweet loss. One less mouth to feed, one less worry. The Sheikh is happy to pay the parents and we are happy to get the job. Everyone is happy."

"The boys don't look happy."

They were filthy, thin, starving. Didn't Master know their stories?

"Dear helper, we feed the boys, clothe them, give them shelter, train them to be jockeys. We are saving children, we are saving their parents."

Munna squirmed. Back home, he had heard outrageous stories of survival—fathers cutting off their children's limbs to turn them into little beggars who would invoke pity in the streets and bring back money.

They stopped at the house and climbed out of the truck. Munna hurried after Master.

Master turned around and looked at him. "Look," he said. "I want my helper to be happy. Soon you will be the Master of this ousbah." His cracked lips curled into his typical smile. "The Sheikh wants to win the Gold Sword. Always other tribes have won it. If you help me win this race I might be tempted to pay you an allowance."

Munna did not want to be Master. He looked at the prickly cacti that flourished in the desert. Like them, he thought, he would try to survive here.

Master went on: "The race takes place end of December. Two months is all we've got." He sidled up closer to Munna, pinning his death glare on him. "Waste time and time will waste us." He pulled out his dagger from under his belt. "Time is this dagger. If you are not quick, it will cut you." He continued, "Lose the race and you'll be my slave forever. So make up your mind."

After the evening meal, Munna flopped on the sand outside the shed, the voices of Ma and his sisters echoing sweetly in his ears, the scent of jasmines in their hair strong in his head. He felt as though he had left his legs back home, his dream of getting out of here seemed so hopeless.

The sunset melted and darkness fell suddenly. Trembling, he pranced back and forth, slapping his arms against his shoulders to keep warm.

Soon the stars shone, a few at a time, all over the black sky. He stared at the heavenly transformation of the night sky now speckled with millions of stars, the galaxy of *Akash Ganga*, the River in the Sky, looming over him. He made out the seven bright stars in the shape of a kite, the Big Dipper, and the upside down kite, the Little Dipper. The stars were so bright and seemed so close, he could almost reach out and grab them. How could they shine so bright and cheerful when his future looked so dark and distant? The gods were mocking him for sure.

A thin sliver of moon appeared. It sailed slowly across the night sky, sharp and curved like the Master's dagger. Munna fled inside the shed.

Racing Season

The racing season turned Munna nocturnal. His day began at three in the morning when the sky was dark as dried blood, and it ended when the red sun fled to the dunes. The season would last until the grand finale, the Gold Sword Race.

Nervous about oversleeping, he turned into a desert owl, keeping watch all night, checking his watch every few minutes. In the middle of the night, at the stroke of three, he made sure that the trainers attended to the camels. Then with the pressure lamp in hand, he went to wake the camel boys, watching out for snakes and scorpions lurking in the chilly darkness. Inside the filthy tin shack, the boys lay on the floor, legs curled up to their chests. Babur sucked his thumb noisily. Munna felt hesitant to wake the kid up so early. He had to. He began to sing the Hindi song his mother sang to wake him up, "*Re mamma re mamma . . .*" and Babur's eyes opened.

The boys sat up, scratching their sleepy eyes, hair tangled. Within seconds, fighting broke out.

"Aw! He pulled my hair!"

"But he kicked me first!"

"Eeee. He's lying!"

At three-thirty while the world still slept, Munna led the

trainers and the boys, now on the camels, in a single file, the lead rope tied to the nose peg of each camel, their bellies rolling from side to side, all the way to the Al-Salaam Racetrack. The sandscape was awash with the light of the full moon, a lustrous pearl afloat in the velvety darkness, the camel shadows dancing on long distorted legs on the sand. The sleepy little souls slumped on camels were dead to the world. Akber's song rang in his mind. "Nobody wants us. We are d-e-a-d. We are bhoot bacha, ghost boys." Indeed, they were the Ghost Boys.

Upon their arrival, the racing track was lit up. Master surfaced, striking his stick at the puny little legs of the boys if they yawned. He snapped his fingers at the trainers and they ran to his truck and returned shortly, carrying a pile of racing implements which they distributed to the boys. The trainers then *kushed* the camels, who duly sank down on the sand on their knees, groaning. The boys dismounted. Master checked that the camels were well saddled, then commanded, "Mount them."

Omer and Amin hung the walkie-talkie sets around the boys' scrawny necks and hoisted them onto the camels. Master explained to Munna. "They stick to the saddle with Velcro. Less chance of falling."

One camel had no rider. Babur was missing. But among thorny bushes, a bit of his t-shirt stuck out like a blue flag. Amin went and pulled him out, and he ran to Munna, clinging to his ankle, whimpering, "Help me, Bhaiya."

Munna watched helplessly as Master dragged away the kid by the arm, picked him up, and dropped him on the back of his camel.

"Ma, Ma, I want my Ma," cried Babur.

"Shut up! The camel is your Ma," said Master.

Master raised six fingers. "Six jockeys, six camels, six

races. Each jockey rides a different camel. Clear?"

"Yes, Master-ji," said Munna. He did a quick calculation. The racing track was fifteen miles long. If the camels ran an average speed of thirty miles per hour then each practice race would last thirty minutes.

Master raised his stick to start the race. The trainers hit the hind legs of the camels and they rose like sand hills. "Bismillah!" the trainers shouted, hitting the camels' legs again, and the beasts cantered away across the sandy track, the terrified boys screaming, tearing Munna's heart apart like paper.

"The louder the screams, the faster the camels run," said Master. "Come, helper, we'll chase them by car." They sat inside the truck. Master drove on the outer tarmac track, chasing the jockeys on camels, monitoring every swing of their gallops, honking and yelling in the walkie-talkie: "Faster, faster. Whip them. Harder, harder." The whips whirred as the boys whacked the camels.

When the race came to a close, Master drove to the finish line to receive the jockeys. Much to Munna's chagrin, the first boy was Akber. Master patted the boy's back. "Good job. You'll eat with the Big Boys." He looked at Munna. "Akber's our best jockey."

Babur came in last. Munna lifted the dejected boy off his camel and kissed his cheek.

"No coddling," warned Master.

The next practice race began as the sun broke over the horizon, painting the sky a pale shade of pink. It was hard to believe that this same sun would later turn so relentless and burn them.

Master handed a notebook to Munna. "Jot down the timings of each race," he said. "They'll help us make effective decisions for the big day."

Munna checked the time on his watch. The first race had lasted an hour, but it included the prep and the break. Still five more to go. But as the races progressed, it took longer for the camels to complete the circuit because unlike horses, camels are clumsy. They would cut across in front of each other or run in zig-zags instead of straight. Some of them, like the slow Shenu, would turn around and head back to the start. Also, camels don't steer well. Approaching corners, they often bumped into each other or against the railings. Sometimes they suddenly sat down, as if to say they had had enough. Then the jockeys whipped them.

The races went on until noon, when the sun blazed like a ball of fire. On their way back to the ousbah, Munna and the trainers led the train of weary camel boys, each of them clutching the reins of their equally weary camels, casting little shadows on the sand. In sheer misery, they plodded across the sun-scorched sand. Sweat ran down their faces, attracting strange-looking insects that sucked at every molecule of moisture.

The Sandstorm

Fridays at the ousbah were quiet, as there were no races, but for Munna the day was anything but quiet. A bank of clouds clothed the sun yet he was sweating rivers as he stood in Master's backyard over Babur's crouched body. The boy's round face peered out between his matchstick legs. Earlier, Babur had tied Tiger to a chair with camel reins and eaten his fish. Crime with a capital C.

The enraged Master had brought out his stick, when a blue van pulled up in front of the house. A tall white man in jeans, boots, and hat stepped out of the van, looking typically like a cowboy in the western comics Munna had seen. Master thrust his stick in Munna's hand. "Six strokes," he said and left to meet the visitor.

Munna held Master's stick, feeling the rush of hot blood in his hand; the stick was meant to discipline unruly camels, not children. A feeling of helplessness tugged at his heart. He had become too fond of the little one. He glanced toward Master's house. Was Master watching them from his window? What would Master do to him if he didn't mete out Babur's punishment?

"I sorry, Bhaiya," said Babur, his body twitching, expecting a stroke any time.

"Shut up!" said Munna, then regretted it. Something

93

came over him and he flung away the stick and broke into a sprint across the sandscape. *Run, run, run away*, urged a voice inside him. He had no idea where he was going or what he'd do. All he wanted was to get away as far as he could. He had hardly run for ten minutes when his heart threatened to give and his lungs heaved. The sun shone relentlessly. Sweat poured down his face and back. Everywhere around him was sand. *The hungry desert will eat you*, Master had said. He stopped to catch his breath. Watching the rocks and the sand around him an unease came over him. He turned around and started back toward the ousbah. But a hot wind was now blowing against him, roaring, tearing at him, stinging his face. Dust clouds whipped and whirled like devils all around him. He would never make it.

A few feet ahead of him something moved. The blowing sand made it hard to see. It drew closer. Surely, it wasn't . . . What in the world was Babur doing here? The little boy pressed his head against Munna's body.

"Bhaiya, you run very fast."

"Babur, why did you follow me?"

"Master-ji smell irifi, sandstorm. I scared you die."

Munna looked up at the sky. A turmeric-stained dust cloud was speeding his way, rushing across the sand and eating up the sky with the deafening roar of a freight train. Munna bent down, tied Babur's scarf over his face, keeping open only a slit for his eyes, and did the same with himself. Then he gripped the little hand. "See that shelter," he pointed to a rocky promontory about twenty yards away. "Let's run for it."

They ran as fast as they could, the hot howling wind blasting in their ears, chasing them like a pack of djinns, until they reached the rocky outcrop. Munna pushed Babur into a crevasse, then he himself went in, entering a small cavern. They removed their masks. Babur's face was white with dust, Munna laughed. "You look like a ghost," he said. "Close your eyes," he said, and blew the sand off Babur's face.

"My turn," said Babur.

Munna shut his eyes and Babur did the same to him. Outside, the wind screeched and howled like a demon. Babur dug his fingers into his ears. Munna snuggled the boy against his chest, feeling the frantic heartbeats of a scared sparrow, the boy's breath warm against his own face. "Don't be scared. A giant outside is shaking a mango tree and the mangoes are falling, thud, thud. So many mangoes."

"What's mangoes?" asked Babur.

"A nice, sweet fruit," he said. "My best."

"Mine too," said Babur. 'My bestest."

"Dear Babur."

Munna's hand felt an object in his pocket, among his marbles. He took it out. The pen, with the compass at its head.

"Master-ji's pen," cried Babur.

"I . . . borrowed it," Munna said. "This compass will help us find our way back when the storm ends."

"Can it find my Ma?" Babur shook Munna's arm.

"I don't know," Munna said, hopelessly.

Babur caught hold of Munna's arm with unexpected tenacity. "Bhaiya, please don't leave me," he said in a squeaky little voice, and nestled his head upon Munna's shoulder.

A Head Storm

Back at the ousbah, to his immense surprise, Munna received a hero's welcome. Babur's crime had been forgotten. The trainers performed acrobatic stunts, arching their backs and bending their knees until their toes touched their heads, while the camel boys cheered. Master beamed, pulling Munna into an embrace, murmuring under his breath: "I looked everywhere for you, praying for your safety in the storm. In God's name where were you?"

Munna stood tongue-tied, failing to come up with an excuse.

"Ah, I get it," said Master. "You chickened out didn't you?"

Munna began: "I went for a walk . . ."

Master's face darkened. He smacked the back of Munna's head. "*Bewakoof!* Fool! You tried to run away? I told you the desert's a hungry beast. Spare me the grief of burning your pyre."

Munna didn't mind the crude remark now that he and Babur were safe.

"Disgraceful! I make you the head of the ousbah, give you shelter, good food . . . and this is how you repay me?" The blistered lips welded together. "Didn't your parents teach you to appreciate your host?"

Munna was offended but stayed calm. He put on his game face. "I'm sorry, Master-ji." He bent down to touch the man's feet, the Indian tradition of respect for elders. When he straightened up, Master looked visibly moved. He raised his forefinger. "Take me one step ahead, my boy, and in the holy name of Lord Ram I'll fly a hundred more for you."

That night another storm brewed, this time inside Munna's head. A head storm. Hot wind gushed against his ears. He held his head, heavy as a melon about to explode. Yes, he had made headway in his plan to escape, but what would he do about Babur? Fate had cheated the boy, stolen his childhood and happiness. The brave boy had risked his life to warn him of the sandstorm. Now it was his turn to save his little brother. If he left the ousbah, who would help Babur when the others bullied him? Besides, Master didn't like Babur. Munna didn't have the heart to leave the kid behind.

But he had to return home. He had promised his family that he would bring back a lot of money. They must think he had forgotten them just like his father had before.

He went outside and stared at the darkness for an answer. It was a beautiful, clear and starry night. Suddenly he realized that he felt calmer. There was no longer a storm in his head. He now knew what to do.

Back in the shed, he found his shawl, nuzzled his cheek against it, feeling its softness, pictured Ma knitting it. How well he knew the rhythm of the clicking needles: knit-purl, knit-purl, knit-purl, stitching her love for him. The shawl was the only tangible memory he had of his family, but Babur had liked it. Munna folded the shawl, took the pressure lamp, and left for the tin shack.

Inside, he caught sight of the curved form of Babur lying

on his sack, his stick-thin arms and his stubborn chin prominent, as he sucked at his thumb. "Psss," Munna whispered,
spreading the shawl over the curled body.

The boy sat up, rubbed his eyes. He looked at the shawl
spread over his legs, fingered the soft silkiness and squealed
in delight.

"You can have it," whispered Munna. "It's yours."

Babur held the shawl to his nose, breathing deeply, and
Munna's heart soared. He squeezed Babur's bony arm.
"Shhh. You'll wake up the others."

Babur kissed the back of Munna's hand. "You's my bestest Bhaiya."

Munna smiled. Perhaps Babur had other brothers. Munna
might be the only one who cared for him, but to him, Munna
was the world.

In the shed, he despaired. His plan was to escape from
the ousbah. Now, Babur had muddied it. He hoped that
his gift to the little boy would assuage his guilt, free him to
move on.

Story Time

The racing season proceeded as scheduled. The practice races at the track were long and grueling, the days short and punishing. At noon, the sun shone with all its fury. The heat rose off the sand and shimmered like waves.

It was day twenty-six since his arrival at the camel farm. Munna sank like a sack on the sand outside the stable, exhausted. Sweat streamed down his body, soaking his *kurta*. He was zonked out, but still there were chores to do.

Mentally, he assessed the progress of his escape plan. 1. He could now climb on Shenu's back without hesitation. 2. He had hidden some dates and a few water bottles in the storeroom. 3. He still had to get back his passport.

His worry now was Babur. He did not have the heart to abandon the boy when he was subject to constant bullying. If he could bond with the other boys, he could nudge them into accepting Babur.

A few feet away, the trainers were grooming the camels with scrub-downs. A hard, bristled brush first loosened the dirt off their backs down to their legs and under their bellies; the second time, the brush flicked off the remaining dirt; in the third brushing their skins were stimulated to produce natural oils; finally, a softer sponge cleaned their faces. Amin told silly stories in Arabic to Omer, who doubled up with his *kik-kik-kik* laughter.

Munna recalled the magic of story time at home when Didi read to him and his sisters at night. He'd snuggle up to Ma and listen. Surrounded by his family, he felt absolutely safe. As he mused about his home, a sudden thought came: he could tell stories to the boys, make them happy, slowly ease them into accepting Babur as their little brother.

Quickly, he finished his chores, grabbed his camel book from the shed, and ran to the shanty, followed on his heels by Amin and Omer. Sticking two fingers into his mouth, he whistled. The trainers, in a bid to outdo him, blew louder whistles.

"Story time," cried Munna. "Who wants to hear stories?"

The boys shoved each other out the tin door, crying "Me, me, me," as though he were handing out sweets.

Akber sneered. "I don't want to hear silly stories." He stamped his foot in the sand, kicking up a cloud of dust, and stomped away. The rest of the boys gathered around Munna under the tall date palm across from the stable. Babur fussed and fumbled with his new shawl, adjusting it around his shoulders, eyeing everyone around him with pride.

Munna opened the book to the title: *Little by Little the Camel Goes into the Couscous.* He changed it for the boys to *The Foolish Master.*

The boys giggled, chanting the title repeatedly. Their laughter was like a happy song to Munna's ears. Except for the haughty Akber, he had always seen the boys as terrified, reluctant to sit on the camels, fighting among themselves. Now seeing their smiling faces filled him with a warm glow.

He read aloud: *One day, Master-ji and his camel set off across the desert. Soon night came. Master tied his camel, pitched up his tent, and went to sleep.* Munna inclined his head on his shoulder. Babur pulled his shawl over his head in a bid to copy him, Mustapha whispered something to Smiley. The word spread and the boys sang: "Babur's a girl! Babur's a girl! Babur's a girl!"

"I biiig boy. I brave boy," said the indignant Babur.

"Shush!" Munna said, and the story time resumed.

Now the wind began to blow. The camel, who was tethered outside, grew cold, so it thrust its head under the flap of the tent and said: I'm freezing. The sand is choking me. I can't breathe. Please Master, can I come inside?

The boys gazed wide-eyed at Munna.

But the tent was small, so Master said: Put your head inside. So the camel put its head inside the tent. Soon the wind grew fierce, and the camel said: Please, can I come further inside? Master said: All right, but there is room for only two legs. So the camel put its forelegs inside the tent.

The boys laughed again, their excited faces urging him to continue.

In the middle of the night there was a sandstorm. The camel pleaded to Master: Can I put my hind legs inside the tent? The Master nodded, too sleepy to argue.

Mustapha leaped to his feet, jumping aimlessly in excitement: "I know, I know what happens." The others shushed him, urging Munna to continue.

And so the camel came inside the tent, kicking Master-ji outside in the sandstorm like this.

The boys burst into laughter and a boisterous cheering broke out. Munna was pleased. Storytelling was better than acting. He promised to tell them another story the next day. Everyone left, but Babur, who tugged his sleeve. "I likes stories, Bhaiya. Pleeese tell me again."

"It's time you went to sleep," said Munna.

Babur didn't. His bony arms twined around Munna's

hips, clinging to him. He whispered, "I gots a shhecret."

Munna tensed. "Get off me," he said. "You're choking me."

Babur folded his arms, and thrust his lips out, sulking.

Munna melted. "Fine, tell me," he said.

"I dunno. I forgets," said Babur.

"Want a tickle fight?" Munna said. He tickled Babur under his neck, behind his ears, and in his sides, laughing along with him, talking silly, singing gibberish.

Babur laughed so hard, he fell on the sand, tears streaming down his face.

"Okay, your turn," Munna said.

"Close your eyes," said Babur. Munna did so, peeking through his fingers as Babur plucked a branch from a nearby shrub and brushed it lightly on Munna's arms, down to the soles of his feet, until he laughed and was reduced to tears as well.

Exhausted, they drew closer and butted their foreheads.

"*Bhoot aur Buddhi?*" Foolish or wise, asked Munna.

"*Buddhi, buddhi*," replied Babur.

Finally, Babur got up. He took a few steps, then spun around, flashing his trademark toothless grin. Then he scooted off.

Munna knew right then that he had been taken. He would delay his escape plan and take care of the boy first. The harder he tried to act on his plan, the closer Babur got to him. Like the camel in the story.

The Canadian Girl

It was Sunday. Munna was hanging clothes in the washing area when he saw Master with a couple of visitors outside his house. Munna recognized the tall cowboy figure he had seen before. At his side was an equally tall girl with electric-blue hair. She wore ripped jeans and a baggy blue shirt. All three stood beside a van. Munna's mind raced. What if he hid in the van? Where would it take him? Where did they live? He had been to the Sheikh's palace and the racing track, but he had not seen any homes. He saw Master struggling to remove crates of camel feed from the van and went over to him.

"Master-ji, I can help," he said.

He began to unload the crates. Behind him, he felt the girl's gaze upon him as he carried the crates to Master's house. A furtive glance over his shoulder revealed that one side of her blue hair rose up into spikes; the other side looked frightfully messy, as if she had just rolled out of bed. He looked away. It was rude to stare at girls.

His job done, he sneaked a look at the strange girl again, hoping she wasn't looking.

She was. She smiled at him and he felt he had inhaled the intoxicating scent of *champa*, the blossom of joy that made one's head spin. Embarrassed, he looked away again.

Master introduced the visitors: Mr Hadwoker, a famous Canadian scientist, worked for the Sheikh. The scientist gave Munna a hearty handshake, putting him at ease at once. "Glad to meet you, young man." He cuddled the girl closer to him. "My princess," he said with a mischievous glint in his wrinkly eyes.

"Aw, D-a-d," the girl protested, pulling away from him. She turned to Munna. "I'm Avra," she said, standing a head taller than him. The piercings in her ears and nose glinted in the sun, as she fumbled to free the knot of the camera strap around her neck. She looked at him. "I'm sorry. You are?"

"Munna," he said. "I am Munna, assistant to Master-ji."

"Munna as in the moon?" she asked, her dark eyes wide open.

Munna smiled and rubbed his chin, feeling the prickly stubble along his jawline. In the past three weeks he had shaved only a few times. He had never worried about it before. This girl had made him conscious of his looks.

"I'm scrapbooking a journal of my days here. Do you mind showing me around?" she asked.

His gaze flew to Master for approval.

Master nodded, and said to him in Hindi, "Stay clear of the brats," a redness spreading across his cheek like a rash. Munna was delighted to discover Master's soft spot.

He and Avra made for the stable. Munna kept his gaze down on his scuffed slippers, feeling awkward as his white kurta flapped about his legs, while she clomped jauntily at his side in boots, the camera strap swinging around her neck, her shell necklace clanging.

"Hey Munna, are you like related in some way to Master?" she asked.

He shook his head firmly.

"I'm sorry. I could have sworn you have his eyes. Big and dreamy."

He scowled. *Master has the eyes of sin.*

She bit her lip, then pointed at his kurta. "Cool toga. It's what ancient Greek scholars like Socrates wore. Actually, your bandana and steel hoop make you look like a pirate." The stud on her brow shone. "Excuse my curiosity and pardon my language, but why the hell would a hunky pirate, of all the places in this whole wide world, come to Dead Man's Land?"

He smiled, admiring her ability to keep her sense of humour in a place like this.

His hands curled around the marbles in his pocket. The only girls who had ever praised him were his sisters. At a loss for words, he felt himself blushing and looked dumbly at her.

"Hey, I might look wild, but I don't bite."

He faked a smile.

"Mind if I take your picture? Mother will be thrilled to see a teen manage a camel farm."

He hesitated, but she adjusted her camera, viewing him from the lens. His gaze slipped to her long slender hands holding the camera. Strange, she wore a ring on each finger. Stranger still, each nail was painted a different color.

"Smile," she said, clicking the camera as he caught a glimpse of her tattooed wrist. The pattern looked like a bird.

"Doesn't Master freak you out?"

He shrugged. "You get used to," he said.

"Dad admires the man. Says his burns are honor scars, and his ugliness hides beauty. Poor guy, I can't imagine being him. People get scared of his looks."

He pursed his lips. If only she knew how heartless Master

was. He had to be careful. She and her father were Master's friends.

"Munna, do you like it out here?"

He cleared his throat, and looked down at his dusty plastic slippers. What should he tell her? He hated it here, absolutely hated it. The relentless sun sucked the life out of him. He was depressed by the conditions of the boys. The sand made him itch like crazy and he feared the creepy insects. He missed his home.

"It's okay," he said, kicking at a stone in his path. "You?"

"Can't wait to get back, but got to put in time for my crime."

She blew her disheveled bangs out of her eyes. *Crime?* He looked at her queerly. *Did she say "crime"?*

"No chance in hell of a parole until Dad's Falcon project is done. Beats me how I'll survive five months of hell."

He failed to understand her desperation. Why was she upset if she was here for a short time? She had her father. She'd jump out of her fair skin if she knew about the Ghost Boys.

When they reached the stable, he led her to the camel pens. "Rani," he pointed to the sleepy white camel.

"Wowsers!" she cried, clicking her camera joyously several times. "She's expecting, right? Malika can't wait to see the baby. She's named her Iman. You met Malika, right?"

He nodded. The princess must have mentioned him.

He showed her the other camels: Dilu, Tasha, Rozy, Nuri, Shenu, Kismet. "Prized racing camels."

Avra's eyes widened. "Racing camels? You mean like racing horses? Malika didn't tell me that."

Dear Lord. Munna realized his error. *Master will kill me.* Why did he open his big mouth? Didi was right when she said his chameleon tongue flew faster than a rocket.

"Racing shots would be amazing for my scrapbook. I'd love to watch a race."

He needed a distraction. Fast. Seeing the twin chocolate faces of the trainers staring at them from behind the door, he waved to them. "Amin, Omer, here."

They ran over, yelling excitedly, "Madam, golden madam," and curtsied as if she were royalty.

Munna introduced them. Avra asked them if she could take their pictures. The trainers embraced each other, bubbling with excitement. They climbed the rope ladder to the roof of the stable and jumped. They did acrobatic stunts, aerial cartwheels, splits and somersaults, yelling all the time, and posing for Avra.

"Awesome!" she exclaimed again and again, furiously clicking her camera. When it was time to leave, she thanked him. "I'll show you the pictures next time," she said, knocking her fist against his, smiling her intoxicating smile.

He watched her clomp away in her boots back to their car, sorry that she had left so soon.

Still caught in the magic current of meeting Avra, Munna sat outside his shed, staring at the bright moonlight filtering through the cacti and bushes, casting strange shadows. In the distance to the west, he made out the dark wavy outlines of the sand dunes. When he first arrived, the black hills at night stood like menacing sand monsters. Restless like him, they moaned and groaned like troubled sleepers every night. Now their slopes had softened into the sinuous curves of dancers. He could almost imagine the *thak-thak* of a drum and the lilting melody of a flute. When would he see Avra again? He felt he could confide his plan to her—or was it too soon to trust her?

Avra's Place

There were no practice races on Sunday morning. Munna stood outside the shed, practicing his juggling, tossing his marbles into the air and catching them. He was looking forward to riding on Shenu so he could explore the surroundings and plan his escape, when the two trainers came running towards him. "Hu-yaa, Hu-yaa!" they yelled their familiar exclamations. "Master-ji wants you *now*," Amin said. The gleeful looks of the trainers implied that Munna was in trouble.

What wrong did he do now? What did these snoopy fellows tell Master? Pocketing his marbles, he shambled towards Master's house. At the sight of Avra's van, his heart skipped a beat. Had she blurted out to Master that he had told her about the camel races?

Mr Hadwoker leaned against the car door, chatting to Master. No sign of Avra.

"Hello Munna." Mr Hadwoker beamed a smile. "I invited Master to see Avra's pictures on my desktop computer, but he's busy. Would you like to . . ."

"Yes," said Munna before the man had finished and hastened to step into the van when he felt his arm squeezed. It was Master, his nose twitching like that of a camel in distress.

"Don't stick your head out too far," he spoke in Hindi.

"*Goras*, white men, can brew a sandstorm from a speck of sand."

"Don't worry, Master-ji," said Munna, pleased at the man's discomfort.

He sat in the van next to the scientist, feeling like a celebrity. The engine thrummed and a voice came on. *Drive ten miles to the end of the road and turn left.* Startled, he searched for the voice on the dashboard.

Mr Hadwoker chuckled. "It's the GPS. The navigation system tells us how to get about." He pressed a button on the dashboard to shut off the system. "No need for it here. The desert has just one highway."

Munna leaned forward in his seat. "Sir, does the highway go to Deeba?"

Mr Hadwoker nodded. "But we are heading east towards what we call the compound."

Munna felt a heady excitement. He could hardly sit still. Forget Shenu. The van was *uttam*, the perfect getaway vehicle. If only he knew how to drive! He cleared his throat: "Sir, how does the GPS work?"

Mr Hadwoker said that satellites up in the sky relayed information through rays that were captured on the monitor. These rays were like light, but they were invisible. "We use GPS in falconry too. We implant microchips—little objects—in the Sheikh's falcons and they send us information, and thus we can track them down when the Sheikh and his party go hunting."

Munna was impressed.

They turned into a paved road that cut through a long stretch of sparse bush and scrubby undergrowth. The sun was high in the sky but it was cool in the van.

"So, young man, what brings you here?" asked Mr Hadwoker.

"My job," said Munna, cautious not to say a lot since the man was Master's friend.

Mr Hadwoker said, "You look way too young to be working. You should be in school."

Munna shifted uneasily in the seat, fumbling the marbles in his pocket.

"Anyhow, Master says you are doing a great job. Avra will be glad to see you. The desert can be a pretty lonely place for teens."

Munna nodded.

They climbed a hill, upon which stood a cluster of buildings. "See that?" Mr Hadwoker pointed to a tall glass building. "The Falcon Centre," he said. "We monitor the Sheikh's hunting from here, while the falcons hunt small birds called bustards thousands of miles away in the farms in Cholistan."

Munna sat up, intrigued, his mind churning. Some of the camel boys came from Cholistan and Uncle's farm was there too. Uncle had bragged that a rich Sheikh had paid him millions to lease his dry farm. Very likely the farm was filled with bustards.

They slowed down and approached a pair of tall iron gates. Mr Hadwoker swiped a card over a panel in the pillar, and the gates swung open. They drove into a luxurious green area. Rows of red-brick villas stood around a circular cobblestone compound. Bright desert blooms gave off the heady fragrance of cinnamon-spice.

"Many foreigners who work in Deeba live outside the city in this compound," said Mr Hadwoker. He parked the car in a garage beside a row of houses. "We have tennis courts, a gym, a playground, and a few shops and cafes."

Munna nodded, wondering why Avra felt lonely with all these luxuries available.

They passed a wading pool filled with brightly colored fishes, then went up a few steps into a cool house. The scent of fresh baking evoked in him memories of home-cooking. How long was it since he ate a *jalebi?* Crispy, sweet, and orange, dripping with syrup.

"Munna's here," Mr Hadwoker announced and slipped into an adjacent room.

Avra sprang to her feet. She was wearing a baggy blue shirt over ripped jeans, which seemed to be the same as before, its threads dangling above her knees. Her camera swung around her neck. "Ahoy, pirate of the desert," she said with a grin.

This time he had a comeback. He bowed slightly. "At your service, Princess."

"Don't," she gave him a light, playful kick on his leg, and he winced, pretending it hurt him.

They sat side by side at the dark wooden table on which lay a scrapbook, a sparkly pen, two tall glasses of lemon juice, and a plate of biscuits. Across the wall, a brass-framed photograph showed a young Avra in a swimsuit, standing between her parents on the deck of a boat. Munna's mind conjured up a photo of his own family, in which he stood with his three sisters around Ma and a blurred figure—he had forgotten what his father looked like.

"Hey! I've far better pictures to show you." She clicked the keyboard of the computer and the monitor filled up with images, all titled *The Hungry Dunes*. A reddish sky arched over the dunes.

A succession of images showed minute-by-minute a sunset in the desert, the sun like a ripe golden orange sinking behind the sand hills.

"Nice," he said.

"Have you been to the dunes?"

111

He shook his head.

"Dude, you must. Yogi took me." She mimicked her father's voice: "*Avra, the desert is magical and mysterious—the more you look at it, the more you see there's a lot going on.*" She added, "He was right, we heard the dunes sing. Dad said the wind made the sand grains vibrate. Too bad my camera couldn't capture their song."

Munna was intrigued. So the cries of the trapped maiden he heard every night were caused by the wind.

"I used to think the desert is for oddballs and weirdos, but I admit, some of the beautiful sights tipped me upside down, inside out, turned me into a freak of nature."

He frowned. For him, the stark silence of the desert amplified his loneliness. He was stuck here in a limbo, between his home and the ousbah, between heaven and hell, neither dead nor alive. The only good was that he liked the camel boys and Shenu, and now, this girl.

She showed him other photos. Click. Himself floating in his white *kurta*. *Pirate of the Seas of Sands*. Click. The trainers showcasing their acrobatic feats. Click. The camels in the stable. Click, click, click. She flicked past multiple images of eyes. "I'm obsessed with eyes," she said. "Some people read tea leaves, I read eyes. Every pair of eyes tells a story. Here's the prettiest eyes of all. Want to guess?"

He stared at the sad almond eyes and knew he had seen them.

"Malika," she said. "Sometimes the prettiest eyes are the saddest." She flicked over several images. "Hey, look at this photobomb." She zoomed on a blurred image on the screen entitled *Tarzan-boy hanging on a vine*. An animated face peeked out from a branch of a thorny tree.

Munna grinned. It was Babur.

"You know him?"

"His name is Babur," he said.

"Babur who?" Her studded brow creased and her eyes narrowed. He tried to keep a straight face. "A little boy," he waved dismissively. "Tell me, what do my eyes say?"

She gazed into his eyes for a few seconds. "Hmm. Right at this moment, I'd say fear. Try reading mine?"

He studied her face.

"Sparkly," he said. "The sparkle in your eyes makes the stars jealous."

"You're a poet! You'll have no trouble winning the heart of any girl." She winked. "Fancy doing farm work. Do you like it?"

"I . . ." he began then paused to evade the question. "I did quite well in winning the heart of a camel or two at the ousbah." He smiled.

She twisted her rings around her fingers, then picked up the sparkly pink pen from the table and began to chew it. They looked at each other for a few odd moments then exchanged smiles. "Aw!" She dropped her chewed-up pen. "Time for real food, eh?" She pushed the plate of biscuits near him. "I baked them."

He nibbled the biscuits, the chocolate-bits melting in his mouth. "Nice," he said.

"Credit to Mother's no-fail-recipe," she said. 'But she can be a royal pain. Guess what she sent me for Christmas?" She didn't wait for him. "A stuffie!" she shrieked. "Can you believe it, a stuffie for a fifteen-year-old!"

He didn't know what a stuffie was.

"I'll show you," she said, and left the room. Quickly he slipped a biscuit into his pocket.

She returned holding up a foot-long stuffed bear in a Santa hat. "Meet Teddy." She shook the bear and the button-blue eyes fluttered open, then closed; it could wink, blink, and roll its eyes. She pressed a button on its back and it laughed. She dropped it on the table and it cried.

"Mother reckons I'm still a baby."

"You'll always be a baby in her eyes," he told her, knowing how Ma and his sisters had always coddled and cosseted him, much to his annoyance, since he was the youngest in his family. Now he missed them. "You're lucky," he added.

She rolled her eyes and leaned forward. "My folks are up in my face," she whispered.

Could life be so bad for a girl who had everything?

"Long story short, I was caught smoking ganja at my friend's party. Oh brother! I was grounded and shipped out here. So here I am!"

He smiled. She's a wild one, daring and rebellious like Kismet, he thought. They were two totally different species. Like parallel lines that don't meet. He ought to give up his fantasies. Get real. Duty before dreams. Loyalty before love.

"Your turn," she said. "Tell me your story."

"Father's dead. My Ma is one of the best cooks in my town. It's called Guj and it's in India. I have two beautiful sisters older than me."

"What's your fire, your passion?" She kissed the camera strung around her neck. "Mine is photography. I plan to be a journalist. You?"

How could he tell her that he wanted to be a famous movie star? He was a cloud walker. "A cricket player," he said. He was a good batsman in his school team, after all.

"Cool. You must explain the game to me. In Canada, ice hockey's the rage."

"If you explain ice hockey to me," he told her.

"Deal." She knocked her fist against his and the bear fell. She picked it up and sat him on the table. "Sorry, Teddy. Your mommy's mean. She doesn't want you." She made a motion to throw the bear.

"Don't. I'll take him."

"Seriously?" Her dark eyes widened. "What will you do with a stuffed bear? Or is it for someone?"

"Um . . ." He seemed to have fallen into a fox hole. "For the boy in the photo. Babur."

"Tarzan? You mean the tree boy in the picture?"

He nodded, when Mr Hadwoker surfaced. She ran to her father. "Dad, my scrapbook's going to knock off my teacher's socks." Her father put an arm around her and winked at Munna. "I gather you were helpful," he said.

"Awesome!" she said, flashing her megawatt smile at him and a jolt of adrenaline ran through him all the way to his tingling fingers.

"Ready to go?" Mr Hadwoker looked at Munna.

Munna nodded. He packed the bear into its box and followed the man into the car. On the way, Mr Hadwoker told him he was welcome to visit his home whenever he wished. "Avra can sure do with the company."

"Thank you, sir," Munna said, but he knew Master would never give him the opportunity if he could help it. "Avra's a smart girl," he added.

He and Avra might be two parallel lines that would never meet, but the fragrant *champa* blossom made his heart sing and dance. If only she knew how to drive. When he reached the shed, he saw Babur wandering about. Seeing him, the little boy came running.

"Bhaiya, where you go? I looks and looks for you everywhere," he said. He hugged Munna around his waist. "What you got?" Babur looked at the box in Munna's hand.

"Two presents for you." Munna took out the chocolate-chip cookie from his pocket. "Here," he handed it to Babur, who grabbed it and began eating it.

"Your second present." Munna opened the box and took out the stuffed bear, and gave it to Babur.

Babur held the bear and giggled. "He gots no teeth, like me."

Munna showed Babur how to make the bear's eyes open and close, and how to make it laugh and cry.

Progress With the Passport, and Riding a Camel

The following week, Munna waited eagerly for spa day. The camels had to be groomed in preparation for the trial race, which would be held soon. That would give him the opportunity to search Master's house again for his passport. When the day finally came and Master and the trainers left with the camels, Munna headed to Master's house. He had already checked the kitchen and bedroom last time, so this time he made a beeline for the suspicious-looking wooden chest in the hallway, from which Master had found the spare clothes for him.

Reaching it, Munna pulled open the top drawer. Tunics and scarves. The second drawer: files, pens, and notebooks. The bottom drawer: letters, and a thick brown envelope.

He emptied the envelope. A stack of different colored passports fell out—Mustapha, Hassan Khan, Akber, Ali Khan, and then, aha! his. Munna Patel. A blue booklet with the three lions on it. A shiver of delight ran through him. He held the passport close to his chest. Where would he keep it? Certainly not in the shed. Master was bound to search it. His glance fell on the window and he stared outside. The sun lit up the backyard with its cactus hedge. He knew where, he would bury his passport right in front of the man.

Pleased with his ingenious idea, he went to the kitchen and double-bagged his passport to protect it from worms. Next, he ran to the stable, found the scoop for dung removal, and returned to the backyard, where he searched for the ideal spot. There was a variety of cactus plants that formed the hedge. A few had leaves shaped like human hands, with thorns on them, others were long and ridged, a few bore beautiful pink and yellow flowers. A ball-shaped plant with an orange cap caught his attention. *Uttam*. Perfect. He counted his footsteps to the back door of the house. Sixty-six. The devil's number. Their *chawl* back home too, had sixty-six stone steps, sixty-six teeth in the mouth of his curse. He'd better finish his job before Master returned.

He dropped to his knees by the orange-cap cactus and with some effort, because the earth was dry, dug a hole big enough. He placed the bag inside and filled the hole with the sand and said a small prayer over it. He would unearth his passport when it was time to leave.

Back at the ousbah, after the day's practice races and his stable chores, Munna found himself alone. No longer did Babur totter after him. The little one was busy being Teddy's father.

"Shall we go for a ride?" Munna asked Shenu and led her outside by her rope. He made her *kush* and mounted her. She rose to her full height of seven feet. He kicked his heels lightly at her flank. "Go on, Sweetie."

Off they went, at first in awkward fits and starts, stirring up clouds of dust. When she was steady, he pulled the reins to the right and she cantered along the sandy path parallel to the highway to Deeba. They reached the metal fence and stopped. At last, the thought. When he was ready he would exit the gate on Shenu and ride for about four hours and hit Deeba.

He pulled at the reins and returned to the ousbah, confident that he could leave in a few days.

Rani's Baby

Back after the dreaded practice races, Munna flopped on the hay-lined floor of his shed, exhausted, when a shadow fell over him.

Shenu!

Swinging her head and gangly neck, she drew closer to him, flaring her nostrils to sniff at him. Then she sank to her knees, locked her dark datelike eyes into his. All the aches in Munna's bones melted away. "Hello," he said softly, stroking her back. Shenu nuzzled against his hand. Excited, he took off his scarf and tied it around her neck and found himself singing to the camel in a soft voice, making a few motions of a dance. He stopped and they eyed each other.

"Okay?" he said.

After a moment, as if agreeing, Shenu stood up on fours and slowly ambled away.

In the dead of the night, Munna awoke to a foul stench. It was the smell of blood, he recognized it because in Guj he would often pass by a butcher shop. There came a moan. He shook the trainers awake and they followed the stench to Rani's pen in the stable.

Rani lay on her side on the floor of the pen in a pool of blood, moaning, her chest rising and falling with each breath. Blood dripped out of her rear. She was in labor. But why was she bleeding so much? Munna told the trainers to look after Rani and ran to alert Master.

"Hai Bhagwaan!" cried Master. "The Sheikh's most prized camel . . . nothing should happen to her." He made a quick call on his mobile phone to the camel hospital, grabbed a first-aid kit, and hurried along with Munna to the stable. Inside Rani's pen, the trainers trembled, frantic with fright.

"Out," Master said, dismissing them. He knelt on the blood-splattered floor and stroked the bleeding camel. Blood ran over his hands but he didn't seem to mind.

Within minutes, a veterinarian arrived in a green surgical gown with two assistants. They proceeded to put on masks and gloves, and one of them removed a clean plastic sheet, upon which she placed some surgical instruments. She handed a large spoonlike object to the vet.

"She's stopped breathing," said Master's anxious voice.

The vet bent over Rani and put his stethoscope on the camel's chest to listen to her heartbeat. "Erratic. Irregular," he pronounced. Munna's view was blocked, but he heard snippets of information: *Baby's too big; breech calf; uterus rupture*. It sounded serious. There was a flurry as an assistant quickly shaved the hair off one of Rani's legs. The vet wrapped an elastic band tightly around the leg and inserted a needle into a vein. Then he hooked the needle to a tube attached to a plastic bag of clear fluid and taped the needle securely in place.

Finally with Master's assistance, they hoisted Rani on a gurney and wheeled it to the long camel ambulance. Master left with them, leaving Munna behind to clean up the mess.

Later in the day, Munna found a beaming Master, back from the camel hospital, crooning to his cat: "Where is my

Kitty Litty?" He cuddled the fat creature with the tenderness of a mother and turned to Munna. "Rani has a baby girl. They named her Iman." He clapped Munna's back. "The Sheikh's happy. Your quick alert saved Rani and saved our hides."

Munna was happy too, especially for the princess.

Baby Iman

The stable was abuzz with excitement, Master couldn't keep still. Mother Rani would bring her newborn baby home today. As instructed by Master, Munna and the trainers packed down Rani's pen with thick fluffy layers of new rice hulls and shavings to make a deep litter for her and the baby's comfort.

The long white ambulance pulled up outside the stable. A man in a long white Arabian robe opened the back door to let the camels out. Rani knew her way about the stable and trotted gingerly into her pen, her baby fumbling after her. Munna stared at the baby; she was as black as her mother was white, but her tiny feet were white up to her ankles, as if she was born with white socks.

Master put a large blanket around Iman, led her to a corner of the pen, and tucked her in with a look of satisfaction. He glared at Munna. "Stop wasting time on storytelling. The calf is precious. Watch her closely, else . . ." He ran his finger in a throat-slitting gesture.

Munna nodded. Who had ratted on him about the storytelling? Akber? The trainers? He would take care of the calf, not because of Master, but for Malika, the sad princess. To the boys' disappointment, he cancelled storytelling that evening and camped inside the pen while Rani pranced around in circles, a nervous new mother.

The baby slept peacefully, so he read *The Camel Book*, flipping through the pages until he came to the part about newborn camels. *The camel is a mammal that gives birth and breastfeeds her babies. A she-camel remains pregnant for twelve or thirteen months. A full-term baby weighs between 25 and 50 kilograms and is about 90 centimeters high. She stands up within two hours after birth. The mother breastfeeds her baby for a year, after which she starts to eat food . . .*

Did he hear a cry? Yes, the baby was awake. The cries were faint, making him wonder how long she had been awake.

He drew close to the baby. "Hello, Iman, welcome to the world," he said.

Two big fearful eyes blinked in rapid succession. She didn't have a hump. He stroked her. She was adorable. A white line zig-zagged across her forehead. Sign of good luck or bad?

She cried again, this time a high-pitched squeal that stopped and started. She licked her lips.

"Ah, you are hungry?"

She rose shakily to her tiny feet and took a few faltering footsteps towards Rani. He was struck by the miracle. How did the newborn baby know how to walk? How did she know who was her Ma? And that she would give her milk?

To his horror, Rani thrust her pendulous lips out and grunted fiercely, baring her yellow fangs as if to devour her.

The baby whined. "Rest, little one," he said. "Your Ma's tired."

But the hungry baby drew near her Ma again. This time Rani raised a back leg, kicked the baby, and bolted outside. The frightened baby backed up so quickly, she bumped against the wall of the pen, letting out a haunting wail.

Frightened, Munna ran to tell Master, who called the camel hospital on his phone. Within minutes, the veterinary team was back in the stable. The vet examined the baby and turned to Master. "She needs an intravenous transfusion," he said. He wrapped the baby's leg with an elastic band, inserted a needle into a vein and hooked up a tubing attached to a plastic bag with colored fluid. "It contains nutrients and antibiotics," he said. An assistant brought out a crate of milk cans and a set of feeding bottles. The vet instructed Master to feed the baby every six hours. "Rani had a painful delivery and is exhausted," he explained. "She needs time to recover."

But the next day, Rani ignored her baby again and bolted outside. The baby whined, looking lost and forlorn. Munna could hear the baby's belly rumble. He put his finger near the baby's mouth and she sucked it readily. She must be starving. Perhaps he could feed the baby with a bottle. Munna opened a milk can and filled a feeding bottle with milk. He sat on the floor of the pen, pulled the baby towards him, lay her head on his lap, and fed her the bottle. It felt good to hear the hungry baby suckle the milk noisily.

He returned from the practice races the next day to see a number of cars parked outside Master's house. He spotted Avra's van as well. Master was busy chatting with the Sheikh's men and Avra's father. Good. Pretending he had been assigned a task, he picked a pail of water and sneaked into the stable.

Rani's pen was filled with the woody odor of aromatic Oud. Looking ahead, he saw Avra and the princess sitting on a beautiful rug with the baby Iman's head on the princess's lap.

"Hey, Munna," said Avra. "We've been waiting for you."

Munna wondered if he should bow before the princess;

he was shocked at how pale she looked—the color of rice, her eyes ringed with dark circles. He felt for her. He knew the gut-wrenching pain of abandon. She had hardly recovered from her mother's death and now her calf was sick and dying. Grief did not discriminate between royalty and commoners, he thought.

"I told Malika you are good with camels," Avra remarked. "Can you help save her calf?"

Munna nodded dumbly though he didn't know what to do, except to feed Iman with milk bottles. He wanted to help the princess. When he had accidentally broken into the palace ground with the expectant Rani, the princess had risked her father's wrath to help him.

"Thank you, Munna," the princess said in a teary voice.

Her caretaker, who was standing beside the two girls, took out a lace handkerchief from her bag, dabbed Malika's eyes and said, in English, that it was time to leave.

In the next few days, Munna had to manage the practice races without Master, who stayed back to attend to Avra, Malika, and others who visited baby Iman. One day Munna returned from the races to find the calf curled into a furry ball in the corner of the pen, squealing in pain. Rani was not around.

"Hush, little one. I'll get your Ma," Munna said.

He found Rani wandering about outside. "C'mon in, Rani. Your baby's hungry. Go to your baby." He pulled her gently by the rope into the pen.

The hungry baby saw Rani and ran to her, but the mother kicked her. Munna ran to the baby. "I'm sorry, Iman," he stroked the baby's back. She looked at him plaintively, her soot-black eyes limpid and innocent, licking his arm as if he was her Ma. He saw her white ankles again, and a suspicion arose. The baby must be cursed. He knew what it was like to be cursed.

He led Rani near the baby again but she glared ferociously at the baby as if about to kick her. His heart clenched. Rani was out to kill her own flesh-and-blood! A camel in a sour mood is deadly. He grabbed his camel book and flung it at Rani. It hit her leg. Good. He'd shoo her out. It was a dangerous move, but necessary.

Keeping a watchful gaze on Rani, Munna edged back, step by step, to the other end of the pen. He reached the gate and unlatched it. The gate swung open to the scrubland outside. Next, he dug out the sugar cubes in his pocket that he kept for Shenu and offered them to Rani to lure her. As soon as she drew near, he flung the cubes outside. Rani tromped greedily towards the treat. Quickly, he turned and bolted shut the gate.

He ran to the calf. She lay on her side, still and lifeless like a broken toy, her eyes blanched, dilating. "Wake up, baby," he shook her gently.

She didn't stir. He placed his ear close to the baby's belly. Her breathing was feeble, her breath growing faint by the second. "Help!" he cried out for the trainers. "Call Master-ji. Tell him Baby Iman is dying!"

A Stroke of Genius

Not only was Iman dying, but Princess Malika was also getting weaker by the day. No longer did she and Avra visit the baby camel. The ousbah was overhung with an air of palpable fear. Munna felt helpless. Tragedy lurked in the horizon for everybody. Master apprised Munna of the situation. The Sheikh did not want to lose his daughter and had summoned his doctors from Europe to save his only child. They had told him that there was nothing wrong with her, except that she was in grief. Her cure was the baby camel's recovery.

Meanwhile the racing track was a bedlam. Master, a bundle of nerves, yelled constantly, striking the boys indiscriminately; the camels were more ornery than usual, spitting and groaning and refusing to run; the nervous trainers chased their own shadows at night. Sitting outside, watching the dark sky studded with stars, the sand dunes looming like shadows in the distance, the desert trees like dancing ghosts, Munna thought there was no hope. He thought of Avra. Couldn't her father, with all his knowledge of science, help? He could track falcons thousands of miles away using satellites, couldn't he do something about a sick baby camel?

An idea dawned. Later he would call it a stroke of genius. Slowly, he walked over to Shenu's pen. The camel was on the ground, napping, its eyes closed. Munna crouched beside her. "I need your help, Shenu," he told her. He tugged at Shenu's lead rope gently, and she stood up without fuss. He led her slowly towards Iman, who was bundled in a blanket in a corner of the pen. "*Kush*," he said, and Shenu sank to her feet on the floor, as requested. Luck seemed to be on his side, so far.

"See baby, see her?" Munna said to Shenu.

To his utter delight, Shenu sniffed the swaddled baby, thumping her tail. She dragged the blanket off with her mouth, and nudged the baby awake. Iman gave a whimper. Shenu began to lick the baby's face.

Yes! Munna's arm shot up in the air. Shabaash! But the very next second, the baby sat up, her black eyes flighty. She quickly backed away.

"Shall we try that again?" Munna said anxiously.

Iman came closer, nervously, and lay down. Shenu licked her down to her tail, then rose to her feet, as if to say she was done, but the baby now went after her. Shenu sat near the baby again. Munna was so excited, he wanted to shout. "Baby has found a new Ma!" he said, then repeated, as if to confirm to himself, "Baby has found a new Ma."

Quickly, he ran to Master's house and told the man that Baby Iman had found a new mother in Shenu.

Master thumped him on the back. "Good job, Munna. You sure have a way with animals. You may just have saved our hides."

But back in the stable, a sudden dread gripped him. *Hai Ram!* Now he would not be able to ride Shenu to Deeba as he had planned. No way was that possible now. Shenu was the baby's new Ma. Iman needed Shenu. His curse had won after all.

Feast Days in the Desert

The desert gods were smiling. As Baby Iman got better, so did Princess Malika. A calmness came to reign on the ousbah. Munna had now moved Baby Iman into Shenu's pen. Sometimes they came close to each other, sniffing and rubbing noses, blowing breaths. Sometimes they chased each other. Meanwhile, Iman was fed with bottles.

Master was happy. At the racing track one day, he performed his acrobatic stick dance, twirling the stick in the air in one hand then deftly catching it in his other hand. "Lakshmi *agayi*," he said in Hindi, referring to the goddess of good luck. "Sheikh Ahmed will hold a lavish feast to celebrate the return of Princess Malika's health. Sheikhs and kings from other countries will come. You'll be the water-bearer and serve water to the guests."

Munna nodded.

The day before the feast, Munna ran into Avra and her father chatting with Master. The Sheikh had invited them to the feast as well. Avra had come to take snapshots of Baby Iman. They walked to the stable. Avra nudged Munna's elbow. "Hey, I emailed Mother and my friends my picture of you with the caption 'Desert Pirate' and got back a ton of screaming replies." She chuckled.

"Pirates are thieves," he said.

"But the one I know spins magic." She punched his arm and he squealed in mock horror, while his heart did a dance inside him. She praised his talent with camels, saying he was making waves among the royalty. "Malika can't stop bragging about you."

"Really?"

"Really."

Inside Shenu's pen, Iman tumbled across the floor like a furry ball. Avra cried out in delight and went clicking with her camera, even going down on the floor to do so. Once, like a playful puppy, Iman climbed all over Shenu, who nuzzled the baby tenderly and licked her.

Munna and Avra walked back to the car, where her father waited, when out of the blue she asked: "Hey, did the camel derbies start?"

He gaped at her. She waited for him to say something, but his lips were sealed. The less he talked, the less he goofed.

She shoulder-bumped him, "Camel got your tongue?"

"The races got cancelled . . . because . . . because Baby Iman fell sick."

She gave his arm a reassuring squeeze. "No worries. Let me know when they start."

For the first time, he felt relieved to see her leave.

On the day of the feast, the ousbah was transformed in a matter of hours into a *mela*, a fair. Billowing tents of red, blue, yellow, and white had been pitched on the sandscape, looking like a scattering of bright tropical flowers under the sky. Master said each tent served a different purpose: the red tent was for the royals, blue for the security staff, green for the sound equipment, air-conditioners and the like, yellow for the food, and white for the staff. At about five in the evening, the Sheikh's chefs roasted a goat in an open pit, about fifty yards from the ousbah. The camel boys inhaled the smoky scent, and their aching hunger was reflected in their eyes. Munna promised them a feast of their own later that night.

That evening he wore his black pants and blue shirt that he had never worn at the ousbah before and made his way to the site. Thankfully it was cool. He caught the remains of the sun's glory as it slowly sank into the horizon, parting like a queen that had lost her throne, leaving shades of red blood in the sky. Waiters in black pants and starched white jackets now ferried about big trays laden with Arabian specialties: sizzling goat, lamb and beef kebabs, spicy vegetable salads, saffron rice, hummus, pitas, and baskets of fruit. Munna dug his hands into his pockets. They were deep enough to squirrel away grub for the boys.

The sirens were heard as the Sheikh's silver limousine arrived at the edge of the site. Munna and the trainers joined the line-up to welcome the royalty. A fleet of long black cars with flags pulled in behind the Sheikh's car and security guards in dark glasses emerged, and scurried to take up positions along the perimeter of the red royal tent. The drummers beat their instruments, and men in black tuxedos and white gloves rolled out the red carpet for the Sheikh to walk on. Master, clad in his new white *kurta*, then opened the door of the Sheikh's car and announced: "His Excellency, Sheikh Ahmed Bin Mohamed."

Everybody bowed in reverence. As the Sheikh emerged and began walking on the carpet, he was greeted by whirling sword dancers and flower-bearing girls, who threw red petals upon him. The Sheikh looked resplendent in a long black, gold-trimmed robe and white *kaffiyeh*, his headscarf, as he strode along the red carpet on the sand, casting a watchful gaze all around, the light of the sunset gleaming on his face. At his heels came Malika in a long cream gown alongside her stern caretaker. Malika lifted her face veil, scanning the crowd. She smiled at Munna and disappeared inside the royal tent. Next, royal dignitaries of other kingdoms came striding along the red carpet, in long white robes that billowed like clouds, followed by a convoy of people.

Finally, the Sheikh's men arrived, one of them with a falcon perched on his shoulder, followed by Mr Hadwoker and Avra in a long skirt. She waved at Munna, and the trainers yelled, "Madam, Golden Madam."

After all the dignitaries and guests had arrived, Munna and the trainers followed Master into the royal tent carrying trays of water, sherbet, and juice. The area outside the royal tent had been turned into a pavilion, with a red canopy above and spread on the ground with a bright carpet on which were thrown cushions with sequins that sent forth flashes of light reflected from the lanterns in the ceiling. This is where all the guests sat. Munna felt a luxuriant sensation as his feet felt the soft rug under him. The strong scent of the Arabian Oud took his breath away. From where he had come to stand, at one side of the pavilion, he scanned the faces of the audience, looking for Avra. He saw her sitting next to her father, her camera focused on him instead of the Sheikh, who had come into the pavilion and sat on a plump pillow on a low dais, facing the audience. Next to him sat Malika and a row of royal dignitaries.

The drums rolled and a group of men in *dishdasha* robes carrying swords leaped into the air, and upon landing, threw their swords up, catching them as they came down. They were followed by a few veiled women dancing, swaying like the ever-shifting desert sands. Everyone applauded.

A man in a long robe with a long amber rosary around his neck knelt before the Sheikh and recited a *qasida*, a poem of praise, in Arabic. An interpreter translated it into English for the guests. The poem stressed that among the Bedouins, a man's status is not assessed by what he owns but by his hospitality, courage, generosity, respect, reputation, and honor. The audience applauded.

Munna noticed the Sheikh and Malika chatting; they turned to look towards him. Malika pointed. A murmur rose among the audience. Master came and said to Munna, "The Sheikh asks for you." The tray in Munna's hands shook, the glasses clattered. Master took the tray from him.

Munna stumbled toward the dais, which was ten yards away though it felt like ten miles. At every step, his legs threatened to give way. He sensed all the eyes watching him as he went up the steps to the dais. This could not be happening. From the corner of his eye he saw Avra clicking her camera frantically.

Munna bowed before the Sheikh, who caught his arm. Munna kept his eye on the Sheikh's large emerald ring, a signet with some inscription on it, as the Sheikh spoke.

"Malika and I want to thank you for saving Baby Iman," he said in a thick guttural voice.

Munna nodded.

"Sit down. Sit beside me. I want to talk to you."

Munna knelt on the dais, his knees knocking together. He raised his gaze slightly.

"Did you listen to the *qasida* about the Bedouin values of hospitality?" asked the Sheikh.

Munna nodded.

"Reputation is the gem of all our values," continued the Sheikh. "I want to be the best reputed ruler for my people and for that I need your help."

Munna was stunned. Of all the people, how could *he* help the Sheikh?

"I hear you are good with camels," said the Sheikh. "I want you to win the Gold Sword Race for me. It will bring *namoos*, pride to my people. I will reward you well."

How could Munna refuse?

Back at the ousbah later, an excited Master told Munna that the Sheikh had offered them a sum of twenty thousand American dollars if they won the Gold Sword Race. Munna's mouth gaped open in amazement, his mind spinning in roller-coaster madness. How many rupees in his share of ten thousand dollars? His heart beat wildly. Not only would he be free, he'd get his sisters happily married, buy a nice flat for Ma, go to school . . . he could buy the world.

Master squeezed Munna's shoulder. "Helper, we'll seize the moon by its teeth."

Munna nodded, but his guilt bone poked and prodded at his throat. Remorse flooded his mind. The Sheikh's reward was *haram*, earned immorally on the backs of the camel boys. He was as sinful as Master, but what could he do? Munna wanted the money for his family and the best way was to join with Master, sign a pact with the devil.

Arrogant Akber

No longer were Master and Munna arch-enemies. Now they were frenemies, both anxious to win the Gold Sword Race for the Sheikh. But nature abhors a vacuum and a new enemy had emerged: Akber the not-so-Great. At the racing track, when Master went off to arrange something, all hell broke loose with the boys. They became a whirlwind of fists and feet, pulling, kicking, yelling, cursing. Babur sat atop Smiley, who held on to Ajit. Akber shoved Babur. "I'll break your face. Your Ma won't know you." Munna did not have much choice but to threaten to report them to Master and the tangle of boys would come apart.

The lead jockey in the races usually was Akber, but Munna's eyes almost popped one day to find that the runner-up was Babur. Was he dreaming? The stuffed toy that Babur called Teddy, it seemed, was his lucky talisman.

Munna patted Babur's head. "Good job, Babur!"

Babur patted the bear's head. "Good job, Teddy!"

But an angry Akber came forward and thrust his finger in Babur's face. "You cheat! You can't take that silly bear with you. I'll tell Master-ji." He turned to Munna. "I hate you. You always favor Babur. You don't belong here. Go home, Big Boy."

Munna understood the boy's reaction. Akber naturally

feared that Babur would dethrone him as the winning jockey. He put his arm around Akber's shoulder, but the boy pulled away. "Look," he told Akber, "I'm soft on Babur because he's the youngest. You can't snitch on your little brother."

"I can and I will," retorted Akber. "That baby is not my brother." He turned to others and smirked. "Big Boy has become our new Monster-ji."

"Monster-ji, Monster-ji, Monster-ji!" The boys chanted. All Munna's work, to gain the boys' trust, had come apart. Akber was the top dog. The boys followed him blindly. Munna had to win Akber for the sake of the big race. He was the only one who could control the cranky Kismet when she had tantrums. Akber and Kismet made a fine match; together they could easily capture the Gold Sword. Munna had to win Akber over.

Dune Surfing With the Boys

Munna took Avra's advice one day and told the boys they were going dune-surfing. The boys whooped with joy, and Munna was thrilled. Thankfully, Babur agreed that the dunes would make Teddy sick and did not bring him along. Unfortunately, Akber and Mustapha refused to come along.

At about four in the afternoon Munna and the boys set off for the dunes. Their hands shielding their eyes, they sang an old Indian film song, *Come, come, come, my friend*. Ajit, Smiley, Shanti, and Babur scurried eagerly after Munna, the pied piper of the ousbah, albeit a good one. The sand beneath their bare feet was hot, but they did not complain.

In a short while they reached the dunes, rows of rippling sand hills shaped by the wind. Munna picked the shortest dune for them to climb, about a hundred feet high. Barely had they gone ten yards when the sand under their feet gave way and they slid down, laughing and sputtering, their faces grimy with sweat and sand. Up they scaled the dune again, this time reaching higher than before, only to slip farther down. What worked finally was scaling the sand hill sideways on the ridgeline using the rocks as footholds and handholds. Bursting with excitement they finally reached the summit.

Munna stood high on the dune. He felt like he was on the roof of the world, the sun's warm glow bathing him. Avra was right, the desert was magical and mysterious. He tipped his head back, stretching his arms up, up, up, to touch the sky, and it seemed he was floating in another time and space, another universe. He strained his ears to hear the dunes sing. Nothing. In the silence, he was convinced that his arrival here could not be by chance. It must be fated. A higher power had sent him here. And he realized that the desert was growing on him, as it had grown on Avra. It might be frighteningly desolate, but it was beautiful, the vastness was intimidating yet intriguing.

They began their descent. Munna told the boys to curl up their arms and legs and turn into balls, and they went tumbling down the hill, brown balls shrieking in delight, their sand-coated happy faces a stark contrast to their fear-filled looks on the racetrack. They were having the times of their lives and it made his heart swell. These happy faces were worth more than the Sheikh's reward. In his mind, he had won a bigger race by making the boys happy.

At the base of the dune, everyone joyfully ran to him. Impulsively, Munna hugged Ajit, who came first, and a chorus of voices broke out, "Me, me, me!" Everyone jostled to reach Munna, to grab a piece of him, hungry for love and human warmth. Clever Babur crawled under Munna's legs and held fast onto his ankle. Munna locked his arms around the boys' shoulders. They were all so swept up in the moment that they broke into a giddy laughter, when there was no reason to laugh. He wished that Avra could take their picture now, that he could freeze this moment in time and it would last forever.

"Bhaiya," he heard a timorous whisper. It was Shanti.

Munna looked down unbelievably at Shanti, who had

always been silent. Now the boy had spoken his very first words. "You can talk?" Munna said, amazed.

Back at the ousbah later that night, before closing his eyes, he joined his hands and prayed to the gods, imploring them, *If you make little boys, then please don't make them poor. And if you make them poor, then please don't make them camel jockeys, for who will look after them?*

Confession Day

Munna was about to take off on Shenu to practice his riding, when Avra barged inside the stable. She was wearing dark glasses and a baseball cap, the bill flipped backwards. Hooking her thumbs into the belt-hoops of her jeans she said: "Ahoy, pirate! Avast ye mate! I came to divvy up the loot."

Munna did not understand. He smiled at her. Catching sight of the gawking trainers behind her, he handed the reins of Shenu over to them, telling them to take her out to graze. When they were out of earshot, he turned to face Avra.

She said, "Malika told me about the camel races." *She knew, she knew.* Munna's face caught fire. "Chill, we are mates."

Munna was speechless.

"Dad's discovered that when the Sheikh and his party go falcon-hunting in the Cholistan desert, they enlist little boys of poor farmers and bring them back to work as jockeys for them."

Munna slowly shut his mouth, realizing that it had been hanging open.

"Munna, I read dreadful stories on the internet about boys as young as two or three sold as jockeys in camel races.

Here, I printed some for you." She gave him the copies. He looked at them, but he already knew what they said.

Avra put her hand on his arm. He told her about his sister's wedding and how she was sent back, and how she had killed herself. And then everything spilled out. How his uncle tricked him, indenturing him to Master, and how the Sheikh's reward would help his family. He told her about how the boys were starved to keep their weights down.

"I'll show you where they live."

They walked across the scrubland to the shanty. He called out and all the boys rushed out. Akber stood at a distance.

"Boys, this is Avra," Munna said.

The boys stared at Avra. She spotted Babur cuddling the bear to his chest.

"You must be Tarzan boy," she said.

"I, Babur," he retorted in his thick voice.

Avra looked at the boys and said, "Hi, guys. Will you tell me who you are?"

Nobody said a word for a while, just stared at the tall white girl, until Munna said, "Come on—tell her your names!"

Then they all gave their names, except Akber, who stared sullenly back.

"And that is Akber, the fastest rider," Munna said. Akber nodded.

"It was nice meeting you," said Avra, and then she and Munna walked back towards Master's house.

"Mate, we're caught in a sticky muddle, eh," Avra began. "Malika is my friend and her father, the Sheikh, is Master's friend as well as Dad's boss."

"My fault." Munna said. "I'm cursed."

"Aw, don't bash yourself. Bad luck dragged me out

here, but if it weren't for that I'd have no luck at all, 'cause that's how I met you and Malika and bonded with Yogi, my father."

That unlocked a new awareness in him. Thanks to his curse he had made friends with her and Shenu. He had met the boys and given some confidence to little Babur.

"Munna, back home the bad voices in my head said I was dumb and ugly. Solitary confinement here forced me to be my own BFF, Best Friend Forever. Life isn't just finding oneself, it is creating a new self. If I was you, I'd drop the load."

He looked down at his scuffed slippers, which had traversed the length and breadth of the sandscape every day.

She cupped his chin so he looked up at her. "Munna, I'm with you. I bet Yogi will drive you to Deeba, but I need time to make him understand. Let the Hope Fairy in."

He smiled wryly. In his experience, hope was a sweet dish that first made you delirious with joy, then having gained a foothold in your soul, it gouged and gutted your inside, leaving you bleeding. Hope hurt like hell.

"Like my ink?" She flicked her wrist to show her tattoo. "It's a hoopoe bird and brings hope."

"My bird flew away," he joked.

She laughed then turned serious. "Call her back. If there's one thing I learned from Malika, it's that we ought to get rid of the bad, or it sprouts from seed to plant to tree, bearing fruits of sadness.

"Race you to the car," her wild eyes challenged him. She took off her boots and held them in her hands and they bolted across the scrubland.

He let her win. She got into the van and waved him goodbye.

Back in the shed, he mulled over what she had said. She was right. He did carry a load: his curse. The beast always said negative things about him. Did he attract misfortunes because he believed in his curse? Or did his belief in the curse empower it to work against himself? Whatever the case, he was his own worst enemy.

The Trial Race

In preparation for the big race, Master arranged a trial race to be held against one of the Sheikh's other ousbahs. Munna studied his team's racing charts, agonizing over who should ride what camel. No doubt, Kismet was the speediest camel, and Akber the best jockey. Together they made a good team, but recently Babur's timings had grown by leaps and bounds. Dare he match Babur with Kismet? If Babur won the race, he would win the approval of the other boys as well as Master. For the next few days, Munna paired Babur and Kismet in the practice races. No longer did Babur whine about sitting on the camel. He rode with an air of confidence, but with one condition: his stuffie, Teddy, sat beside him on the camel.

A day before the race, the camels and the boys were given nothing to eat or drink. Master stressed that bloated stomachs would give them cramps, but Munna knew better. Master wanted lighter stomachs to increase the boys' chances of winning. Munna showed solidarity with the boys, refusing to eat as well. But when night fell, he raided the storeroom for the camels' food—honey, dates, oats and fresh milk—and sneaked them into the shanty for the boys.

On the morning of the trial race, at the racing track, a nervous Munna checked that the camels were saddled and calm. He helped the boys put on new outfits. The trainers *kushed* the camels and Munna hoisted the boys onto their backs. Everything went smoothly, but when Master left to follow the jockeys in his pickup, Munna heard a cry.

"Babur's eating, Babur's eating!"

Sure enough, Babur's mouth was bulging with what looked like a sucker. Ajit and Mustapha held Babur's hands behind his back while Akber seized Babur's chin, forcing him to open his mouth.

Munna ran over to Babur. "Spit it out," he said.

"Hu-yaaa! Hu-yaaa!" The trainers fanned the fire by gesturing with cutting motions. "Master-ji will cut your tongue."

"Nooo!" screamed Babur, and with that, something shiny slipped out his mouth and fell.

Munna picked it up. It was the Butterfly marble he had given Babur a while ago. He slipped it back into his pocket. "Babur, you can't eat this. It will kill you."

"I thirsty," Babur squeaked in a small voice.

Munna ruffled Babur's head. He put his arms around the boys to gather them into a team huddle. "We are brothers of one team and Akber is your captain. If you want to win the race, listen to your captain." Akber's face glowed with pride. "The race is a one-off event, but brothers stick to each other for life. If any one of you wins the race, then all of us are winners." He glanced at Akber. "Captain, any suggestions for your team name?"

Akber pondered for a minute and said, "The Shooting Stars." Munna recalled his cricket team's cheer in school and taught them the words. An exuberant Akber raised his arm and cried, "We will win, we will win!" and the boys chanted, "One for all! All for one! Woo, woo, woo!" The trainers became cheerleaders, twisting their bodies and dancing in gravity-defying moves.

A referee on the track blew the whistle to signal the start of the race. Munna led his team to the start gate. Babur sat straight up on Kismet, holding on to Teddy. A total of twelve jockeys took part in the race, six from The Shooting Stars and six from the other team.

The referee dropped his flag and the camels took off in a cloud of dust, the masters chasing them on their trucks on the adjacent ring road, yelling orders to their jockeys through their walkie-talkies. Akber on Shenu led the race and Babur on Kismet ran alongside. There was a good chance that one of them would snag a win.

For twenty minutes, the camels remained out of sight. Munna's hand fisted around the marbles inside his pocket. Finally, he heard the thundering hooves of the approaching camels. He ran to the finish line to receive his team. Kismet in the lead spot on the track sprinted like a terrified gazelle in flight from a hunter. But she rode alone. No jockey was on her back. Fear clamped Munna's heart. Where in the world was Babur?

The next three jockeys that crossed the finish line were from the other team. Munna began to breathe fast. Where was Akber? Where was Babur? Why had no one from his team made it? He ran down the track, looking for his boys. He saw Babur's helmet and picked it up. It was smashed. A few yards further, where the looming hulk of Master stood, he saw the boys squatted before a sprawled body on the sand. It was Babur.

Munna knelt beside him, shaking the limp little hand. "Wake up, Babur. Please wake up." He held Babur's wrist, saw that the pulse was weak. "Help!" he cried. "Babur is dying!"

"Cut out the drama," said Master. "I've checked the brat. His head has a small bump. I've called the hospital. God knows why they're taking so long to come."

Of course, thought Munna bitterly. Help would be immediate if a camel were injured. Very shortly, a siren wailed and an ambulance pulled up. Master talked to the paramedics, who trundled Babur away on a stretcher. In his anger and anxiety, Munna approached the jealous Akber and caught him by the throat. "Did you push Babur off his camel? I'll kill you!"

Akber choked. "I swear I didn't. Kismet spooked and Babur fell. As the captain of my team, I gave up my lead spot to help the little bugger."

Munna walked away, shame-faced.

A True Captain

That night at 2 a.m., an hour before Munna usually woke up for the practices, he made his way in the chilly darkness to Master's house to find out about Babur. He had not been able to sleep. After a few feeble knocks on the back door, Munna pushed it open. Curled in the fleece-lined basket by the doorway, Tiger opened one sleepy eye, leapt out, and scurried to the inner bedroom, purring, as if to warn Master of an intruder. After some moments during which there were sounds of stirring, Master showed up, the cat snuggled in his arms. What a frightful sight he looked, with disheveled hair. Nothing like the fearful man Munna knew.

"You better have a darn good reason for waking me up," he growled.

Munna's desperation poured out. "Master-ji, how's Babur? Is he breathing? What do the doctors say?"

"Easy, boy. The brat has more than nine lives. Make some tea, will you?"

Munna filled the pot with water, added tea leaves, and turned back to Master, eager to hear his answers. Munna had come to feel that all the camel boys were his responsibility, they were like his little brothers. Their welfare was important to him.

Master stroked the cat, then looked at Munna and said,

"The brat has a minor concussion. Doctors will observe him for a few days."

Munna was overcome by a flood of relief. He turned back to the stove and lit it. He sure could do with tea himself.

"That brat is always trouble," said Master. "He refused to eat, said he wanted to go back to his big brother."

Munna smiled. Babur wanted what he wanted when he wanted it. "Master-ji, his name is Babur," he said.

Master glared. "Give your heart to kids and they'll chew it. We'll never win the race."

"I don't mind a chewed-up heart as long as the camel boys live," said Munna, and left with his cup of tea in his hand.

Munna found Akber alone by the shanty, playing with sand.

"I like your castle," said Munna.

"It's not a castle. It's a big ousbah with a house, stable, and camel pens." Akber rose to his feet and thrust his chest out. The handsome boy had grown taller and reached up to Munna's shoulder.

Akber Ali Khan, as he had found out from glancing at his passport, was from Afghanistan. "I want to thank you," Munna said. "It was very noble of you to give up your lead spot in the race to help Babur. It takes a noble person to sacrifice for others. You proved to be a true captain."

Akber said, "It was my duty." Then he added, surprisingly, with a wan smile, "I miss Babur. It's boring without him."

Munna returned the smile. "Being the oldest jockey, you must miss your home?"

"I've no home," said Akber. "My step-ma doesn't want me. Besides, one day I will be the Master of this ousbah." He put his arms on an imaginary steering wheel in front of him and let out a noisy vrooooom as if he were driving Master's truck.

Munna felt a pang of sympathy for him. As the trainers would say, he and Akber were same-same. Akber was hurt because his family had turned against him. Munna was hurt because his curse always worked against him. They hurt others because they were hurt themselves and felt helpless. That was why Munna used to play Barrier. Akber was what Munna had been in the past: angry, broken, and a bully. Munna resolved to find a way to help Akber.

Everyone Has Sad Stories

Master stepped out of the bathroom, water from his wet white hair dripping over his forehead. He walked as if in pain, his hands on his hips pressing his lower back to relieve the tension there. Wrapped in a white towel, he looked weak and vulnerable. Tiger purred. Master scooped up the cat in his arms. "We have visitors, Kitty-Litty." He looked at Munna and their gazes locked. Beside Munna stood Babur.

Munna said, firmly, "Master-ji, we came to get Babur's shawl."

"Yes," said Master. "Yes," he repeated. "The brat says you gave it to him. Is it yours?"

"It was a gift," Munna said.

"Who gave you the gift? Tell me."

"It doesn't matter," Munna said. "It was a long time ago. I can't remember."

They stared at each other in silence.

"Master-ji, the shawl," Munna reminded the man.

"Yes, yes, but please don't give it to this brat."

"The shawl was mine. Now it's Babur's. Babur can do what he likes with it."

"You took my shawl," said Babur, pointing an accusing finger at Master. "You's a thief. Bhaiya, cut his hand."

Munna squeezed Babur's hand. "That's not a nice thing to say to elders," he said. He accepted the shawl from Master and wrapped it around Babur's shoulders. He took Babur's hand and they left with Tiger purring softly.

During a break in one of the races, Master mentioned to Munna that he too had lived in Guj, after which issued a volley of questions: "Where in Guj did you live? What's your father's name? Tell me about your family."

"Master-ji, my family await anxiously for the money you owe me for my hard work."

That riled the man. Clearly, he was on a fishing expedition to find out more about him. He would not make it easy, though he wondered why the man was suddenly so curious about his past.

With just two days to go for the big race, Munna told the trainers to put on a show of shadow puppets for the boys, so he could clean the racing implements. Soon the stable filled up with the boys' laughter, delightful sounds of a bubbling brook. Munna gathered the saddles and the cleaning supplies and sat at the stable entrance, when he caught sight of Master trudging towards him. He looked troubled, the smooth half of his face crinkled into a parched old map about to tear. Munna went on with his job, stripping the fittings from the saddles, undoing the buckles.

Master cleared his throat. He locked his arms across his chest.

Munna dipped the sponge into a pail of water, scooped a bit of saddle soap, and rubbed the sponge in small circles over the surface of a saddle, making a light lather. Master hitched a leg up on the stone next to Munna. "I'm trying to get in touch with your uncle, but he seems to be out of town. Would anyone in your family know about him?"

Munna shook his head and went on casually with his chore. Master had been acting funny recently, he thought.

"You can use my mobile to call your family." Master persisted.

Munna dipped the saddle in the clean water in the pail. "Master-ji, my family does not have the luxury of owning a phone. That is why I took up this job." He picked the next saddle and scrubbed it hard and fast, struggling to remain unperturbed. "My family anxiously waits for the money you owe me for my hard work."

"Ask your uncle, I paid a fortune to get you." Master scratched his nose. "I studied your suggestions for the race. I believe the wild brat on the wild Kismet is a match made in heaven. They can snag the Gold Sword."

Munna looked up fiercely, gritting his teeth. "Master-ji, I will not put Babur's life at risk again. Kismet is cranky. Only Akber can handle her."

"My dear boy, these brats are wild and unruly. We must fight fire with fire."

Munna squeezed the sponge in his fist until no more water dribbled from it. Like a cricket bowler, Master was trying to knock his wicket, but he would defend it. Silence hung precariously between them as they looked at each other, struggling to read each other, trying to assert power. In that interim, the laughter from the boys in the stable seemed loud.

Master gave an exasperated sigh.

"I guess you do want to go home," he said bitterly.

"The camel boys are my brothers, Master-ji. They are growing before our eyes without their parents, without adequate food or love. Imagine being betrayed by the very people you love. Imagine being lonely, lost, broken . . ."

Master's hand shot up to stop him. "*Bas, bas.* Do you

154

think it's easy to be charred meat? Everyone has sad stories. We live on earth not heaven."

"Master-ji, buying children, making them work, starving them, is a sin."

One half of the man's face flushed red. "So is poverty, boy. You forgot the poor fathers who can't feed their families. Should they sell their boys or turn them into beggars—chop their arms or poke their eyes out to attract donors? One-word answer: *Majboori*, Helplessness." He threw his hands up in the air. "The poor don't have the luxury to choose morals. When you're as old as me you'll see the very fine line between sin and virtue, finer than . . ." He plucked a white hair from his head and held it up and blew it. "Our nation's father, Gandhi-ji, said poverty is one of the worst forms of violence."

Munna's words slipped out in retort, "Master-ji, one can justify any crime. I'd rather be poor and happy than unwanted, unloved, and uncared for—that is more violent than poverty."

Master's temple pulsed as he glared at Munna. "Listen to me, Smarty, listen well. I'm a father. Every father wants the best for his children. Do you know how useless a father feels when he cannot provide for his family?"

Munna said nothing. His own father had left him.

"I roamed the alleys of Guj like a rat, begging for work," said Master. "Do you know a father's pain when his children are living on scraps of food?" He exhaled noisily, a weary old camel about to be slaughtered. "You be the unfortunate father. Will you let your boys die or offer them a better life?"

"I'd never sell them," said Munna.

"That makes two of us," said Master. "Unfortunately, life doesn't offer you a platter of sweetmeats. It's not as if I got to choose between almond or coconut *barfi*. Sometimes the choice is between bad and bad. Jump into the sea or into the fire. Because of my accident, this is the only job I could get. At my age, winning this race is my last chance, which makes it yours too."

Munna's answer came fast and short. "Master-ji, I'm as desperate as you to win this race, but I will do it the right way. The safety of the camel boys comes first."

Master's jaw tightened and Munna heard what sounded like the crunching of the man's remaining decayed black teeth. He picked up the next saddle to clean but the water in the pail had turned dirty. He needed to refill it.

"Helper, you have a great future. Don't throw it away." Eyeing the dirty water in the pail, he added: "Don't throw the saddle out with the dirty water."

"Master-ji, my future lies in returning to my family as soon as I can."

"*Acha*, Good, I hope your little brothers don't let you down." Master's mouth twisted into a sardonic smile. "Remember, if Sheikh Ahmed loses the Sword, we lose the cash." He paused. "Of course, we both know how much you love being my slave forever, *na?*" he taunted and stomped away, leaving behind a trail of deep footprints in the sand.

The Day Before the Race

The trainers burst into the stable with Avra at their heels, her eyes aglow. "Munna, we're coming to your race, we're coming to cheer your team," she cried. "Credit to Malika." She made a face. "The bummer is, I'm not allowed to take any pictures."

He brought her up to speed about his confrontation with Master.

She squeezed his arm. "Regardless of winning or losing, Yogi's offered to give you a ride to Deeba." Her smile turned into a devilish grin. "Actually, I should bet on you losing the race. It will give us more time to hang out together."

It was his turn to make a face.

"Chill, mate. I'm kidding. Are you nervous about tomorrow?"

He shook his head. If only she knew.

"How's Tarzan boy?"

"As happy as a butcher's pup nibbling on free bones."

"Hey, I brought some goodies for the boys."

Munna called the boys to the stable. Avra opened her backpack and took out a tin of chocolate-chip cookies and fresh lemonade packs. They had a grand feast. She gave a box of crayons and books to each boy. "This is your Dream Book. You may draw your dreams."

Munna said they could draw whatever their hearts desired.

The boys set to work. Mustapha drew a plate of assorted sweetmeats in many colors; Ajit, a bike; Smiley, a ball; Shanti, a kite in the sky. Akber sketched a truck that emitted whirls of smoke. Babur drew a tree with fruits of every color.

"What's that?" Munna asked

"Mango," said Babur. "My bestest."

Finally, Avra pounded fists with each boy to wish them luck. When it was Babur's turn, she tried to hug him, but he wriggled away. "Hey, I'm Munna's friend," she said. Babur's gaze flew to Munna as if to seek confirmation, and he nodded. "She gave me Teddy," he said. Babur's big brown eyes dilated and he glanced across at the door as if planning to escape.

Avra crossed her ringed fingers and said. "Break a leg."

"You breaks your leg," retorted Babur, making everyone laugh.

Munna clarified. "Avra does not want Teddy back. She wants to wish you good luck for the race tomorrow."

"Right. Teddy looks happy. You're doing a great job looking after him."

Babur buried his nose into Teddy, then giving a toothless grin, he stretched out his bony fist and pounded it with Avra's.

The Gold Sword Race

On the Big Day, a blue sky gradually emerged from the east, but in the west, a dark brooding dust cloud looked ominous. Munna twitched all over, in his temple, under his eyes, in his belly, as he led the trainers and the boys on their camels to the Al-Salaam Racetrack. He could not control the outcome of the race, but he was resolved not to show his emotions. Along the way, Akber, the captain, chanted with gusto: "We will win, we will win, the Shooting Stars will win!" and the boys echoed him.

In a special area inside the entrance, a number of brand-new cars gleamed like shiny toy vehicles. They were to be given as prizes. A guard watched over them.

Omer and Amin stared longingly at the new cars, pointing to this one and then that one. "Friend, which one you likes?" Omer asked Munna. "Yes, which?" asked Amin.

"None," said Munna, the guilt bone pressing his throat. The race could be a killer. The jockeys risked their lives to win the race, while Master and he and others desired to win money and cars. They were gambling on the lives of the boys.

The stadium bustled with the pomp of a fête, Arabic music blasting from loudspeakers, and flags of various Sheikdoms flapping in the warm breeze. The Sheikhs in long white robes and black head cloths greeted each other by rubbing noses. Above the tall watchtower, the electronic clock indicated the race time: an hour from now. Munna told the trainers to check the camels and went to look for Avra.

On his way, he ran into young jockeys from the other ousbahs leading their muzzled camels, hoof beats pounding the ground. He eyed his rival team: The Busters. Their Master struck his boys' heads. Whack! Whack! Whack! "Fair or foul, get me a win." The brute made Master-ji look like a gentle goat.

Munna ran past the canteens, where the scent of frying onions hung in the air. The women were cooking for the dignitaries. Munna worried. Last night the boys and the camels were given laxatives to purge their stomachs, and they hadn't eaten since. A crowd of men were staring in rapture at a glass display case. Inside, the famous Gold Sword lay shinning on a bed of red velvet. Munna's fist closed around the marbles in his pocket. *Please make Akber win the race.*

The grandstand looked upon the racing track; on the other side was the stage, and above it was mounted a big white screen. The racing track was ten miles long, and the audience could only view the first hundred yards and the last hundred yards of the race; they followed the rest of the race on the big screen.

The grandstand was split into three: the first section was filled with the Masters of the ousbahs. The middle section, boxed in glass with red carpet, was for the royals, who sat on leather armchairs, each with his own small TV monitor. Among them were the Sheikh and Malika. The third section was for expatriates and spectators, in which Mr Hadwoker sat head and shoulders above others. Next to him was Avra. She waved a victory sign at Munna.

He waved back at her and returned to his team. The boys looked smart in new blue t-shirts, their numbers printed in white at the back. Each wore a helmet, carried a whip, and a walkie-talkie around his neck. He yelled the team's cheer at the top of his voice and they responded, "One for all. All for one. Woo, woo, woo!"

The trainers *kushed* the camels. Akber sat tall and dignified on Kismet. Everything about Kismet—her strong chest, long gazelle legs and fiery spirit said, *I'm the best.* Babur sat with his stuffie, Teddy, on Shenu.

Munna led his team across the arena. The music stopped. The Masters of the five competing ousbahs scrambled into their trucks, which they would drive alongside the race track, yelling orders to their jockeys via their walkie-talkies. A camera man in the back of a truck filmed the race and projected the images on the big screen. Jockeys in red, blue, green, yellow, and purple t-shirts sat on the camels lined behind the string of flags at the Start Line.

The band played the national anthem, followed by a poet who sang a *qasida* in Arabic, praising the Sheikhs. A reporter named the thirty camels in the race and gave past statistics. Munna noted the top five contenders against Kismet: Aisha, Duniya, Jamilla, Najma and Zarin. There was no mention of their jockeys.

The drums rolled. The audience whooped. A voice spoke on the loudspeaker: *"Bismillah! Let the Gold Sword Race begin."* Munna tensed, a sitar strung too tight, the slightest pull could snap him apart, one wrong move from anyone in his team and . . . The referee's gun cracked devilishly loud, sucking all the air from Munna's lungs. A race official cut the string of flags to start the race and the camels surged forward. They thundered down the track, their necks bobbing through clouds of sand, their thudding hoofs echoing Munna's heartbeats. Soon his hair was falling over his sweaty brows, his palms and feet were covered in sweat. A couple of camels paused, one sat down. Zarin, one of the top five, hit her shoulder against the railing. One contender eliminated. Now Aisha led the pack, followed by Duniya, Jamilla, and Kismet.

"Go, Akber, go!" Munna cheered. Three more camels sprinted past, then Shenu came along. "C'mon my *chamak*, my flashy girl! Go, Babur, go!"

Soon all the racing camels were out of sight, and they followed the race on the big screen or their provided monitors. One jockey lost his balance, slid from his saddle, dangling precariously as the camel sprinted. A flash of yellow. Munna shuddered. But not his team, who were in blue. Two camels on the track ran so close, they bumped into each other. One of them was Najma. Munna cheered.

Aisha and Duniya still led the race, followed by Kismet. Farther down the track, Jamilla suddenly spun around, and started running back to the start line. *"Jamilla has gone home to sleep,"* the commentator joked. The audience laughed. Munna cheered wildly. Another contender eliminated. Now Kismet took the lead, sprinting fluidly, hump erect, long neck arched for victory. *Look at Kismet*, said the commentator. *"I will not be outdone, she says."* Munna whistled piercingly loud, almost blowing out his vocal chords.

The camels were now close to the half-way mark, but dust clouds blocked the view. When he was able to see, his heart caved in. Aisha and Duniya were back in the lead, neck to neck. Kismet had slipped back to third position, then fourth, fifth, sixth. *No, no, no.* Akber was doubled over Kismet as if in pain. Munna's world darkened. Akber was the best jockey. All was lost, it seemed. *Loser*, the curse hissed.

The big screen showed Shenu picking up speed. Whoa! She sprinted past Aisha. Within minutes, Shenu was just three camel lengths behind Duniya, the leading star. The camera showed a close-up of Babur clinging on to Teddy. Munna's heart leaped with delight but then Shenu took the far turn out of the racing track, poor Babur struggling to regain control. But he managed to straighten Shenu and return to the track, the audience cheering wildly when, no, no, no, she bolted out of the track again, disappearing from the screen. Munna's nerves crackled like mustard seeds in hot oil.

With less than a hundred yards to the finish line, Shenu reappeared like a ghostly spirit. Not only did she regain her position, she flew like a winged camel, closing on Duniya, the leading camel. Excitement leaped from the commentator's voice: "*Unbelievable. Shenu's back after her wild ride. You've got to believe in miracles.*"

The audience turned raucous, screaming and cheering for Shenu. Munna's mind, a sizzling sparkler at Diwali, exploded in a frenzy of mad delight, as he stared at the big screen, stupefied. What in the world had come over the gentle dove? Why was she so charged?

"*Watch out! Shenu is sweeping into lead. She's flying faster than the wind. She is flying for her life!*"

Munna recalled the trial race—Kismet had been spooked and ejected Babur, but the camel had sprinted on without a rider. Ah! The magic was Teddy. The stuffed bear's shrieks, as Babur squeezed it, had egged Kismet on. Now it was egging on Shenu.

"*Look at Shenu, the power house. Unrivalled! Unequalled! Invincible!*" The excited voice rose: "*The last fifty yards, forty, thirty, twenty, ten, five.*" Munna saw flecks of frothy saliva flying from Shenu's mouth as she crossed the finish line,

Babur flashing his gummy-pink grin. *"Ya Salaam! His Highness Sheikh Ahmed wins the Gold Sword!"*

The people sprinkled rose petals and saffron on Shenu in a tempest of cheering. Munna laughed and cried, his happiness overflowing, tears rolling down his face like a leaky tap. Akber came in fifth. He was leaving behind him a trail of blood as he crossed the finish line.

Munna ran to check on Akber. His bleeding leg had a long gash, but he grinned. "I'm fine," he said. "I'm glad the little bugger won the race."

Munna tied his scarf around Akber's calf. Akber reported that in the last quarter of the race, two Busters had corralled him while a third slashed his leg with a knife, but he had rode on.

Munna saluted Akber. "You're a brave one, Captain Akber," he said. They jostled through the crowd over to Shenu. Munna stroked her. "You turtle, you surprised everyone."

Master came with Babur riding high on his shoulders. "We did it, helper, we did it."

Munna told Master about Akber being attacked. Master put Babur down and left with Akber to report the incident to the officials.

Munna swung Babur up high. "I'm proud of you." Babur leaned into his ear and whispered loudly: "I scared Akber's leg bleed, so I squeeze poor Teddy."

An idea struck Munna. A Big Idea. He could not contain his excitement. He had to tell Avra, right away. Quickly, he put Babur down and sprinted as fast as he could all the way to the grandstand. Mr Hadwoker congratulated him and Avra did a victory dance.

"He won a far bigger race," Munna said breathlessly. He explained his Big Idea. "Teddy's cries egged the slow

Shenu to giddy-up. The jockey was Teddy, not Babur. And, if falcons and vans can have GPS systems then maybe scientists like your dad can make jockeys like Teddy, which means . . . the camel boys can be set free."

"Ohmigod!" Avra's ringed fingers covered her mouth. "Munna, you are a hero."

Munna felt a deep glow of pride inside. "While I hate the curse, it gives me courage. It's like a two-headed beast in my heart. If I lose it, my courage might go," he said.

They fell into each other's arms. He didn't know who had made the first move. All he knew was he wanted to stay in her embrace forever, until a prickly query nabbed his mind: even if he proved Teddy's effectiveness as a jockey, how would he sell the Big Idea to Sheikh Ahmed?

Testing Teddy

In the aftermath of the Gold Sword Race, there was a tidal shift in Master, in his demeanor as well as his gait and spirits. Gone was his arrogant swagger. Gone was his raging lion's roar. No longer did he mete out harsh punishments to the boys. The old man stooped like a sick old camel carrying too heavy a load.

Today was Testing Teddy Day. Munna was ready before the glimmer of dawn broke through the porthole window of the shed. Teddy had better work, he told himself. He ran to the shanty and crouched beside the sleeping Babur. He whispered: "Psss. Can I borrow Teddy? I'll bring him right back. You can go back to sleep."

Babur sat up. "I helps you," he said, his dimpled chin jutting out. Munna knew better than to argue. He explained that Teddy would be the jockey in a few camel races. Babur consented. Akber heard the plan and offered to help as well. They went to the scrubland where Shenu awaited. The trainers watched them from a distance. Soon Avra showed up, carrying a big bag.

Babur ran to her, poking the stuffed bear into her arm. "Teddy likes you," he said.

"And I like you," she said and planted a kiss on Babur's cheek.

She turned to Munna. "Guess what? I brought Yogi's video camera." She winked. "Give the movie producer a few minutes to set up the equipment." She took out a tripod from her bag and mounted the video camera on it.

Meanwhile Munna *kushed* Shenu and let Babur strap the bear onto her back.

"Cut," cried Avra, and Munna pushed the button on Teddy's back. Shenu rose to her feet almost immediately and sprinted across the scrubland to where Akber awaited with Shenu's treat of sugar cubes, after which he led the camel back to Munna.

"Awesome!" cried Avra.

Altogether, Munna administered ten mock races. Seven of them were positive, three failed—either Teddy fell or the video didn't work well.

Satisfied, he returned the bear to Babur. "Teddy is the best jockey," he said.

Babur held the bear to his chest. "Teddy tired. I makes him sleep," he said, and left. Munna eyed the trainers. "Go, take Shenu back." Their faces fell and they left reluctantly, turning frequently to glance behind.

Munna and Avra plonked down on the sand. Scooping a handful, she threw it at him, but he ducked, laughing. She turned serious. "Munna, it's strange how everything can suddenly change."

"Because we met," Munna teased.

"Hmmm. So what's next, mate?"

"I have an idea that the Sheikh might bite," he said, pausing to increase her suspense.

"Out with it, mate." She punched his arm and he feigned pain. She punched him again. "Munna, you're killing me."

"Sorry? Who's killing whom? Remember the Sheikh told me at the feast that he wanted *namoos* above all else."

"Right. He wanted to win pride for his people. So?"

"The Sheikh can make history and win international repute," he said. "He can be the first leader in the world to stop hiring child jockeys for the camel races and use robots instead."

"Wonderbar!" She pumped her arm and pulled him to his feet. "I'll show the video to Yogi and Malika, see if she can coax the Sheikh." In a sudden move, she did the most outrageous thing ever. She pecked his cheek and ran away.

He stood rooted to the spot, it seemed for hours, feeling the tingle on his left cheek. Perhaps two parallel lines could meet in the future. He touched his cheek again.

Munna was in his dream world when the slightly ajar door of the shed creaked and a stooped old man with wild white hair caught the door jamb for support. Master. Fat sweat beads gleamed on his upper lip, about to roll down.

Munna frowned. Master was always prim, proper, and in control. Was he sick?

"You," he pointed a gnarled finger at Munna like a gun. "You betrayed my trust. You and that *gora* girl are plotting to remove me as Master. You aimed for my jugular."

Munna shook his head, startled at the accusation. Who had told lies to the man? The trainers? What did they tell Master?

The man drew closer, a breath away. "*Acha*, Smarty. Hear me, loud and clear. I will beat you." He stamped on the floor, crunching a dung-beetle under his foot.

"Master-ji, I'm trying to help the camel boys."

"Help them? My expense?" The voice rose. "You've no business sinking your teeth into my meat," he said. "I spent years in and out of the hospital, struggling to pay bills, then years hunting for a job, then years sweating at this job—now you want to cut off my lifeline."

"I'm sorry . . ."

"Sorry? Sorry will not feed my family." The wet eyes gleamed like shards of glass. "Do you know what it is like to be a monster? Do you know the pain of shame?"

Munna did. He had spent ten years of his life in the shame pit after his father ran away.

Master's voice turned into a mouse-squeak. "People see my ugly scars, not my ugly pain." He heaved with a sudden expulsion of breath that sounded like a sob. "This job is my only chance to redeem myself and you want to botch it."

Munna could only shake his head.

"I wish I had never set my eyes on you." Master raised his double-jointed fist. "If I had the guts, I'd kill you right now." So saying, he spun around and left.

Reward and Farewell

M unna tossed his marbles into a colorful arc in the air then caught them, keeping a close eye for Avra, wondering if their plan with the Sheikh had worked. She came after what seemed like a hundred hours. They walked together to the stable and he told her about Master's breakdown. She assured him that Yogi would smooth things out with Master.

"Okay, my turn. I've got good news and bad news. Take your pick."

"The bad," he said.

"Um, I'll start with the good. Malika saw the video and convinced the Sheikh to free all the camel boys in all his ousbahs. The Sheikh will make an announcement at a news conference tomorrow."

Munna felt like the weight of the world had lifted off his shoulders. Impulsively, he caught her and lifted her off the ground, surprising himself. "Oh! I think I broke my arm," he joked, putting her down, and she pinched his arm.

Inside the stable, he found the pail and the long wooden spatula used to mix the camel's gruel, and played an impressive beat on the up-turned pail. "Avra, this one is for you."

"Awesome!" she cried, when he was finished. "You're a heck of a drummer."

Her words felt heavenly when it struck him that she hadn't told him the bad news yet.

"Hey, you didn't tell me the bad news?"

"Hmm," she said, deliberately taking her time, her dark eyes mocking him, her *champa* smile lingering on her lips. "The Sheikh asked Yogi to head the project to make robot jockeys and he told me he will need your help."

"Seriously? I will return only if you're here."

"Duh! Why else would I ask?"

He looked at her questioningly. "Since when do you like the desert so much?"

She pulled his goatee. "Hey, first things first. You need to get rid of this or your Ma won't recognize you."

They rose to their feet, brushing the sand off from their pants. And when her ringed hand intertwined in his, he rose on his tiptoe and planted a kiss on her cheek.

"Goodbye. How do you say that in Hindi?"

"*Alvida*," he said.

"*Alvida*," she said in her Canadian accent, making him laugh, and clomped away back to the van. Already, he could taste the bitterness of their separation. He liked Indian girls but not the way he liked her. He would sorely miss his *champa* blossom.

Within minutes of Avra's departure, Munna saw a shiny red sports car pull up at Master's house. Two men in head-dresses slipped into Master's house and came out with Master. They got into the car and zoomed away. Why had they taken Master?

Very soon, the trainers ran to Munna and snapped their hands in the air, crying, "Huyya! Huyya!" They told him that the Sheikh would kill Master.

Munna smiled. He knew these fellows well; they loved to

stir rumors. With Master gone, it was an opportune time to attend to his plan. He asked the trainers to clean the stable; he found the scoop for dung removal, and sneaked quietly into Master's backyard. Tiger sat by the window inside the house, watching him. He waved at the cat, no longer scared of it. Sixty-six steps from the house brought him to the large ball-shaped cactus plant with the orange cap. He dug out his passport, filled up the hole, and left.

Later at the house for the evening meal, Master met Munna, grinning from ear-to-ear. "The Sheikh renewed my contract. I will look after robot jockeys in the camel races. Less headaches, *na*. The camel boys will go to their homes. The Sheikh will set up a temporary school for them, and I with the help of your uncle will trace their families. Ah, he gave this for you. Here." He gave Munna the envelope.

Munna's hands closed over it, blood pulsing in his trembling fingers. He took a glance inside. A check for ten thousand dollars. He rubbed his fingers against the check to make sure it was really there. The money would cover his fare back home and his sisters' dowries and more. He felt a sudden lightness within him, as if the law of gravity had changed and he was flying. Finally, he had cracked his curse, and Didi was smiling at him. He would fulfill his promise to his family and the camel boys would go home soon.

Consumed with joy, he wanted to embrace the man, but restrained and kissed the envelope instead. "Thank you, Master-ji," he said.

"Um . . . we need to sort out your passport problem," said Master.

Munna patted his pocket.

"You have it? You do?" Master frowned. "And here I am desperately trying to call your uncle to ask for a replacement passport."

"Don't. He's not even my uncle. The thief ought to be jailed for trafficking in children."

"Suraj is not your uncle? Then how do you know him?"

"Claims he's an old friend of my runaway father," said Munna.

Master's face wrenched in anguish, his neck muscles twitched. "Your father ran away? When? What's his name? Where is he?"

"In hell," said Munna. "The clod squandered our savings and ran away."

Master gasped, sounding frightfully like the expectant Rani during labor. The poor man was a dithering mess of tics and twitches.

Munna looked at the envelope in his hand. His business was done: he got what he came for. There was no reason for him to overstay. "Thanks Master-ji," he said once again, and left.

The Last Day: You Have His Eyes

Munna barely slept a wink on his last night at the Mousbah. He held on to his check, afraid that it might vanish if he fell asleep, frightened also that he might wake up to find that all that had happened was a dream.

It was dark outside when he began to dress up. He pulled up his black pants, but they reached his ankles. He had grown. He'd have to wear the desert dwellers' tunic that Avra called, "Socrates's toga." Wriggling his toes, he struggled to cram his feet into his black shoes. Nope. *Too big for your boots, huh?* Didi's voice teased. He slung his knapsack on his shoulder and made for the stable. Life in the desert might seem barren and devoid of life, but friendship and hope did blossom.

Outside, the air was surprisingly moist and fresh. He breathed the earthly fragrance again. It must have rained last night, a farewell gift from the desert gods. He whistled as he approached Shenu's pen and she came bounding to greet him. She sank on the hay-lined floor and pushed her nose into his solar plexus, gurgling in delight.

"I'll miss you, my humped friend." He rubbed her shoulder and shared his excitement about going home. Avra and Yogi would give him a ride to Deeba, where he'd buy gifts for his family—they would include everything on Meena's long list, and then he'd fly to Guj in an airplane.

"Bye, Sweetie. Look after your baby Iman. Avra will update me with your pictures."

Outside, the pink sky gave him an uncanny feeling, a déja-vu moment, as he recalled the day of Didi's cremation. A new beginning. Did he hear the singing bulbuls or was he dreaming? Ah, it was the giddy laughter of the camel boys being chased by Omer and Amin. The trainers raced to him and kissed him on both cheeks. "Bye-bye Friend," they said and hoisted him up high. When they put him on the ground, the camel boys ran to him. He hugged them all: Akber, Ajit, Smiley, Mustapha, Shanti, and Babur with Teddy. He would miss them dearly.

"Akber is your big Bhaiya," he said. "Akber will tell you stories and look after you." He took out his marbles, pressing a few in each tiny palm. No longer did he need his security beads. By saving the boys, he had saved himself.

Munna choked back a sob and waved as he left them. He would remember these faces all his life, especially little Babur's looking up at him.

Barely had he recovered when Master showed up with Tiger snuggled in his arms. No longer did Munna need to look up at the man. He had grown as tall as him. "Bye Master-ji. It was good to befriend a croc," he joked.

Master put Tiger on the ground and gazed at Munna with stupid delight, the look of divine madness, as if marveling at a prized gift he had received. His crab-hands scaled over Munna's broad shoulders down to his arms as if to check if he was real, whispering: "Chikoo, my sweet chikoo, how you've grown. I'm so proud of you." The man enclosed him into a smothering bear hug and he felt the knobby old elbows and hipbones pressing and prodding into him, as the man leaned into him, wetting his cheek.

"Beta, I'm your Bapu," said Master.

"You . . . you . . . you . . ." Munna's blood seemed to drain out of him. He squirmed away, *no, no, no, please no*, shaking with a choking mix of disbelief and horror, every cell in his body screaming. No way. His father was dead. He had no room in his life for ghosts.

They held each other's gaze, eyeball to eyeball in an awkward silence, neither of them moving or breathing.

"I was the happiest on earth when I first held you. I named you Anand for happiness . . ."

Munna recoiled. "I'm not Anand."

Master pressed his palms together. "Forgive me, son. Disasters bring about gumption in some, wimpdom in others. I left after my accident, because I couldn't support you all. I tried to hide, burrow into holes like the desert creatures, broke every mirror I came across, yet I saw myself in the horrified looks of others. The ghost of my past always stalked me. Alas, I couldn't hide from myself . . ."

Munna seemed caught in a trance. Who was this man who suddenly wanted to enter his life, whom he knew as Master-ji? Not only did he not really know the man—who had been strict and cruel—he had no desire to know him. Try as he might, he failed to reconcile the blurred image of his runaway father with this man facing him. Avra's stark observation flashed back: *You have his eyes.* Yes, they might have the same eyes, but they were strangers.

Master handed an envelope to Munna. "For Ma. Please tell Ma to forgive me."

It was Master's share of the prize from the race.

Munna was at a loss for words. He knew that his mother still waited for his father, had never given up the hope that he would return. He wondered if he could ever find a place for this old man in his life.

Author's Note

Camel racing is a centuries-old tradition in Arab culture. Long ago the camel races were performed on festive occasions like religious holidays, weddings, circumcisions, and the visit of a sheikh. Recently, however, camel-racing has become a multimillion-dollar sport, and with it, child-trafficking increased. Each year hundreds, perhaps thousands, of young boys are trafficked from the impoverished countries of Afghanistan, Bangladesh, Pakistan, Sri Lanka, and Sudan to work as camel jockeys in the Middle East. A report dated October 29, 2009 estimated that 40,000 child jockeys were riding in the races in the Middle East.

Young boys, two to seven years of age, are favored since they are light and their screams incite the camels to run faster. The boys are forced to work from dawn to dusk in the desert where temperatures can exceed 110°F. They are given little food to keep their weights lower. Often they are beaten or abused by the men hired as *masouls*, or masters. The camels, priced at around $1 million or more, are well-fed and looked after; a child-jockey at $40 is cheap and expendable.

The camel race is a dangerous event. Sometimes the boys, strapped on the backs of camels, slip and are trampled or dragged some distance. Often, the injured jockeys are not given medical treatment. If they do well at the race, they could get beaten or be killed by jealous jockeys. Ansar Burney, a human rights activist in Pakistan, has brought global attention to the issue, and his reports on the practice can be found on the Internet. The intervention of UNICEF and the advent of robot jockeys have undoubtedly reduced child trafficking, but there are concerns that children are still being smuggled to the remote areas of the desert. I have taken a few liberties with *Ghost Boys*. The story starts in an imaginary town in India and moves to a camel farm or *ousbah* in the desert in the Middle East. The characters and events in the story are a product of my imagination but based on real life events in the lives of the child jockeys.

Sources

"US State Department Trafficking in Persons Report." June 3, 2005. http://www.state.gov/j/tip/rls/tiprpt/2005/46606.htm

BBC News. December, 2004. "Help for Gulf Child Camel Jockeys." http://news.bbc.co.uk/2/hi/middle_east/4063391.stm

CRIN (Child Rights Information Network) Resources. April 2007. http://www.crin.org/resources/infodetail.asp?ID=12096

Dawn (Pakistan). December 14, 2011. http://dawn.com/2011/12/14/new-laws-protect-women-from-abuse-in-pakistan/

Everblue Training Institute. (2010). *Plight of the Camel Jockey*. Retrieved from http://hubpages.com/hub/cameljockey

BBC News. February 4, 2005. http://news.bbc.co.uk/2/hi/south_asia/4236123.stm

Courtney Farrell. *Human Trafficking*. Abdo Publishing (2011).

http://www.ekantipur.com/2011/12/14/national/new-laws-protect-women-from-abuse-in-pakistan/345523.html

Child Camel Jockeys in the Middle East - Ansar Burney - Parts 1 & 2. https://www.youtube.com.

Acknowledgements

I wish to express my sincere thanks to

My niece, Azra Bhanji, and Teaghan Young for feedback on the first draft eons ago. Shiraz Kurji, Associate Professor, Mount Royal University, for candid comments and encouragement. My writing buddies for their critiques and support:

Allan Serafino

Late Francis Hern

Jan Markley

Susan Forest

Trina St. Jean

Lois Donovan

MG Vassanji for "dotting the dragon's eyes" to make the story come alive and Nurjehan Aziz at Mawenzi House for all her work on the book and her belief in the story.

A big thank you to my family, Mahmood, Astrum, Shaira, and Sameer for their love and support.

Questions and Ideas for Discussion

1. From what point of view is the story told? Is it effective?

2. What is dowry? Why does the dowry system still prevail even though its illegal?

3. Why does Munna leave school?

4. Describe how Munna's curse affects his fate.

5. Characterize Munna's uncle.

6. Why is Munna's mother reluctant to let Munna leave home?

7. Trace Munna's journey from India to the camel camp in the Middle East.

8. Why are young children enlisted as camel-slave jockeys?

9. Why are female camels preferred in camel races?

10. Characterize Master.

11. Why does Munna delay his escape plan?

12. Compare and contrast Munna's view of the treatment of the camel jockeys with Master's.

13. Compare and contrast Munna and Avra. Do you think their friendship will continue?

14. Why do some mothers in the animal kingdom reject their babies?

15. Do you think bad things happen to Munna because he is cursed?

16. Should Munna have cooperated with Master in the Gold Sword Race?

17. Where do the princes from the Middle East travel for the sport of falconry?

18. What is the connection of falconry to the camel-slave jockeys in the story?

19. Why does hunting for the Houbara bustards hold such an appeal for the Arab princes, and why are they keen on poaching them?

20. Who is the strongest character in the novel and why?

21. What character in the novel evokes the most sympathy and why?

22. Explain the significance of the book title. How does it relate to the novel?

23. To what extent does the author suggest that poverty is the cause of child-slavery. What textual evidence is there to support this.

24. Show three instances that foreshadow to the reader that Master is Munna's father.

25. Do you think Munna should forgive his father and accept him?

26. What in your opinion will eliminate the practice of using child-slave jockeys?

27. Write your own conclusion of the story. What will happen to Munna and his family after five years?

You can find out more about the author from her website www.shenaaznanji.com

Follow Mawenzi House:
facebook.com/mawenzi.house
twitter.com/mawenzihouse
instagram.com/mawenzihouse